SCRIBBLES AND SCRAWLS

BETHANY VOTAW

For Malachi

CONTENTS

SCRIBBLES AND SCRAWLS

MY BROTHER

I knew it would be tough. There was always some time of adjustment to follow, and if we were lucky, peace would come. But it would all go to shit again. But that's okay. I let Mom and Dad know that. I told them I knew how it was, and I cared. I didn't understand, and honestly, I didn't care. I just wanted my brother back. After weeks of constant "I miss Jamie," and "When is Jamie coming back?" she gave me the answer I needed.

"James is coming back next week, Ben," Mom said. Always so formal, stoic. She stirred the cream in her tea at the kitchen counter, quickly wiping up the spill. I sat across from her at the kitchen's island. She wouldn't meet my eyes yet. I didn't care how cold she tried to be. I beamed, and she couldn't help but smile too. I thought it reached her eyes. Maybe it was my imagination. For a moment, I felt like a glob of honey sat in the deepest part of my stomach. It was so sweet it made me sick. Maybe she had a honey pit too. My big brother was coming back! I mean, we were the same size—I was tall for fourteen, and he was short for fifteen.

"Ben, I want you to know something," Mom said.

My face fell. I had so many plans for him—with him. Was she going to be strict and hover like a helicopter like last time? Drag us to therapy where we get artificial hits of dopamine and 'we're making progress' promises?

"What's up?" I asked, putting on my best 'I am not disappointed but please don't crush my spirit' face. She read it. *Good.*

"You see, James is sick."

"*Was* sick. And this is the longest he's been gone."

I thought back to the scenes at the park. The accidental bloody noses and the time Jenny broke her collarbone. It made me shiver. Mom worked to keep the color from fleeing her face, I could tell by the way she bit her lips and pinched her earlobe.

"But he's getting better. It'll be different this time," Mom said. I knew she was convincing herself more than me. "We have new rules. We'll make them stick."

My stomach clenched. There were already too many rules. I needed to show him the little holes I dug by the river. I filled them with the best rocks to skip. We used to try and skip a stone all the way across the river. Maybe this was our year.

Mom looked at Dad, who joined us in the kitchen. He took over. This really was big news. "You need to know this; James is sick in the head," Dad said.

"I know." I squirmed. I hated these conversations.

"No." He set his jaw, and I stopped fidgeting. "Look, James did some bad things. He hurt people. He's getting better now, for real this time. But when he comes back, there are going to be rules."

"Like what?" I kept my voice as quiet as the river out back. This was about the kids at the park, the razor-blades stuck in the slides.

Mom's smile was tight across her bony face. Her eye sockets were giant craters. "Well, for one, you won't share a room."

"We don't share a room."

"You know what I mean." She rubbed a hand through her hair. It was perfect and a brand-new shade of copper. Dad eyed the liquor cabinet. The one above the fridge, the one with a lock. The only key hidden in his office desk drawer.

"I know," I said. Jamie had a bunk bed and I used to sneak over, and we'd play games and darts late into the night.

"There will be a strict schedule," she commanded. A buzz in her phone stole her attention. She leaned over the counter like she was carrying the weight of the world on her neck. A modern-day Mother Theresa.

It would last a week before they flaked out, just 'too overwhelmed' or something like that.

"Jamie can't be alone with strangers," Dad said.

I cracked a smile. *Jamie.* Dad was excited for him to come home too. He barely called him that anymore.

Dad rattled off a list of other rules—simple things like Jamie was only allowed to have forks at dinner when Mom and Dad were around, something about plastic cups, and other crap. I stopped listening when my mind took me back to the riverbanks in our backyard. I thought the water started moving faster like it was excited too.

I could already imagine the look on Jamie's face when I skipped a rock across the river. He hadn't even been able to do that, but I'd been practicing. Then I remembered Mom and Dad in front of me and chose to look somber, even a little afraid, but I wasn't. Still, I widened my eyes just a little and frowned my lips so they knew I was serious. But I couldn't wait to skip those rocks.

His hair used to be blond, bright like the sunshine. Now it was like a shadow. I knew he was trying to be angry, but when Jamie walked through the doors, he let a smile slip. I couldn't help but notice how his spine seemed to melt into the couch. It really had been hell since he had been gone. I didn't think Mom and Dad would like me to give him a hug. Instead, I smiled from my assigned seat.

We watched movies after dinner as one big happy family. We all sat on the couch in our "usual spots" Mom had designated for us when we were toddlers. We ate popcorn and pretended this was normal. *Transformers* boomed across the TV. Mom and Dad shared weird looks at the loud noises and violence, it wasn't even that bad. But I wasn't watching anyway. I kept looking at Jamie, hoping his eyes would meet mine.

He held off for a while, but they slipped, and our eyes locked. He set his jaw and shook his head. I tried to be supportive, to look like his friend. I even had my palms facing up, like the counselor told us to do.

But he was always angry.

He looked away, but it wasn't long before our eyes met again. Eventually, he gave me a little smile, especially after I mimicked skipping stones. A piece of happiness he could still recall. His mind was all mixed up now. Like each time he came out, his brain was more Jell-O.

I sliced my hand against my neck, like I was chopping off his head. Or cutting his throat. It only meant he was a loser; it's always been our sign, like a middle finger or something. Then I worried Mom or Dad noticed, but they were too busy pretending to watch the movie, too caught up in pretending this was normal.

I didn't watch the movie; I watched the rising and falling of Jamie's chest as he breathed in and out, in and out. I promised myself to behave, to be extra good so he could stay longer. I didn't want to rock the boat and make it tougher on him.

When the movie was over, we made small talk. I don't remember what, something about how his room was "just as he left it." Mom looked proud of her handiwork, like she was displaying the innocence of Jamie's youth. Holding on to when we were little. She grabbed him by the hand, gentler than I'd ever seen, and lead him to his boyhood room, complete with a football lamp and poster of Batman. The light blue and ironed curtains did nothing to reflect who my brother was. Jamie said something sarcastic. Dad blew out his breath; he had been holding it all night.

I balled my fists at my side. *Not yet, Jamie, just be good a little longer.* Things would calm down. We brushed our teeth, eyeing each other through our reflections in the mirror so it didn't count as staring.

Mom reminded me of "no late visits." I wouldn't bother him anyway, too early to push the limits. Mom locked Jamie in. I wanted her to lock me in too.

Then I heard the struggle and the arguing. Muffled words like someone talking through a pillow. Maybe it was just the walls. Both parents begged Jamie to spare my little brain and heart from any loud argument and distress. Mom's voice went squeaky; Jamie's was a harsh whisper. It made ears bleed.

Eventually, things went quiet. They didn't try to hide anything anymore. Mom sobbed. Dad clicked open the liquor cabinet above the fridge. The sounds of liquid pouring floated down the hall, under my door, and into my ears. Jamie breathed out, long and deep. I tried to do the same.

But I couldn't. So I slipped from my only oasis under the covers and reached into the dark depths of my closet. I found the little shoebox buried under my neatly stacked shoes. It gave Mom no reason to come in and clean up if it was already neat. Everything else was a mess though. My hand got hot when I reached into the worn box. Beads of sweat started at my temples, and I hadn't even opened it yet. The box was worn, and I opened it with my fingertips, afraid the contents would scorch me. The neat pile of bills was stacked on one end, another pile of stud earrings and shiny necklaces on the other. They smiled up at me.

I cradled the neatly organized bills in my hand,

counting them over and over, reliving the memory attached to each bill. This one was from my mom's purse, about two months ago. I got this hundred from grandma's purse last time she came to visit. I stole this earring off a girl on the bus. Her wallet too, but it had no cash in it.

I fingered the bills and caressed the jewelry. And when my heartbeat went back to normal, and I could hear Jamie's gentle snore from through the wall, I could finally sleep.

The morning almost felt normal. There was mention of the previous night's drama. I still wanted to know what it was about. But I came to my own conclusion when I saw Mom switching over laundry during breakfast. Jamie's sheets. I looked at him. He shook his head. He ate his eggs with a fork, sliding the tines over his teeth. The remains of Dad's late-night glass were still in the sink. I could see the fumes of brandy still floating in the air.

Jamie ate slowly. He stared at me. I stared back. Jamie's jaw clenched tight. So did his grip around the fork. I took my dishes to the sink; I even put Dad's glass away. The liquor cabinet was locked. No more evidence of his late-night treat.

Mom kept busy with cleaning our already clean house. I finally convinced her to let us go outside—she even brought us lemonade on the patio. I half expected her to bust out the old cookie sheets and start baking. I knew she wanted to make up for the lost bake sales and parent meetings at school. She told us not to leave the patio, and I felt her gaze pierce us through the windows. I knew she hoped the concrete was enough of a cage. Before the door closed, she was tapping away on her phone, trying to get a hold of anyone who would still listen to her.

"What's it like in there?" I finally asked.

"Like last time, but the food was better."

It looked like it was better. His once skinny body had some squish to it now. His wiry arms were loose and limp. Maybe it was the drugs the doctors had shoved down his throat. His voice wasn't his either. It's like someone also shoved smoke down his throat, and he coughed for weeks.

"I collected some good rocks," I said.

"Cool," he said, taking a giant swig of lemonade. He leaned back in the chair, legs spread like he owned this place.

"My arms are bigger now." I laughed, but I knew I struck a nerve.

He rubbed his head, sunk away from me, and his eyes flashed red. "Doesn't matter," he said. "I'll get back to normal, even with all the shit they're pumping my brain with. The chemicals are melting my mind."

"What do you mean?"

"It wasn't me," he said, gulping the lemonade.

I watched his Adam's apple bob up and down. "But you said you did it."

"Of course I said that. It's one of the steps to get out of that place. You would have taken all the blame and then some to get out of that shithole."

I wanted to ask who he thought did it. But he was right. I would have said all the right things just to get home. Anyone would have. Jamie rubbed his arms like he was cold despite the sweat already dripping down his temples.

We waited for Mom to be on the phone with some other relative and started our sprint. My legs pumped hard over the uneven grass. I jumped over the few large rocks and branches. The grass got greener the closer I got to the water. My lungs burned by the time I could touch the small river. I won, but he might have let me. But he was also panting just as hard as I was. We grabbed fistfuls of rocks and hurled them into the water.

"What happened last night?" I asked, ignoring the pain in my arm from throwing too hard.

"There was piss all over my sheets." He flung another rock. "Mom didn't believe me, Dad either."

"Piss? Are you sure?" I threw another rock, pinching my shoulder. I hid my grimace.

"She could smell it and blamed me," he snarled, throwing his rock short. "I thought it was the cat. She said the cat's been locked up. Whatever. I just needed a bed that wasn't soaked in piss, and it was like I asked them to move the world."

The cat was my fault. We had one before Mom found it dead and skinned under the porch swing. She swore we would never have another, but I begged and pleaded. She thought I was lonely and caved. Now it lived a life locked in the master bedroom, out of "Jamie's reach and temptations."

"Still, are you sure?" I asked.

"Oh, not you too." He hurled another rock. It made a big *splash*.

"What?" I made sure to say it when he didn't have a rock in hand.

"You're like Mom and Dad, blaming me for shit I don't do, making me think I'm crazy. But the stupid thing is." He hurled another rock, and I tried to hide my flinch. "Maybe they're right. I can't remember shit anymore. These pills and medications just turn my brain to mush." He picked up another rock and tapped it against his head. "All that shit about the park? Maybe it was me, and maybe I really am a monster because I don't remember or care anymore."

I nodded.

"How'd you get a phone?" he asked.

The question felt like a slap on the face. My cheeks flamed and burned, and I bit my tongue. I loved the taste of iron anyway. "I don't know what you're talking about."

"C'mon, I hear you clicking away on that thing late at night."

My stomach dropped. It was like he'd stabbed me. "And?" I forced myself to be calm.

"It's a piece of shit. How old is it? And really? In your pillowcase? Easy place."

"It gets the job done." I shrugged. The first-generation smartphone was more than I wanted to spend. I traded memories in the form of bills for that piece of shit phone. I wasn't going to lose it now.

"How'd Mom agree to it?"

I sighed. "She doesn't know. Please, don't tell her."

His surprise was evident by his raised eyebrows. He

paused throwing a stone. "Wow, baby bro finally getting —" He looked at the rock in hand. "Stones." He laughed, and it felt real.

I laughed too. "Yeah, she'd flip." And I knew he wouldn't tell.

Mom's voice interrupted the slap of rock on water. I jumped, so did Jamie. We each threw one more stone, a final act of rebellion. Mine made it farther, but Jamie thought he won. I wanted to argue, but Mom was red-faced and had Dad on the phone. We raced inside and got some lectures; I tried to take the blame. She ignored me.

And the days went on like this. They shifted to weeks. Mom breathed easier despite the still precarious veil of peace. Jamie's cheeks started to get color, and his eyes became less dull. He got in trouble for petting the neighborhood stray dog. Apparently it was against the rules or something. There was a big row about that, but everyone came down for dinner and nothing else was said on the matter.

It was our blissful and ever-shifting peace.

My jaw tightened when I found Dad's signature glass in the morning. I sat at the kitchen island, rubbing my eyes. I had a headache, and Mom went to fetch me Advil. I hoped we had the chewable tablets even though I wasn't kid-size anymore. They were grape and felt like chalk in my mouth. I threw in a cough for good measure. Jamie squinted at me.

Mom handed me a glass of water, no pill though.

"We're out." Her face was pale. She stood across the kitchen island from Jamie. She tapped frantically on her phone, her red nails clicking over and over and over. Jamie rolled his eyes, hopped over the back of the couch, and flipped on the TV. We watched him watch cartoons, neither Mom nor I are willing to pull our eyes from the back of his head.

He sat in the wrong spot, Dad's spot. I swore I could see the bile rise up in Mom's throat. Her green insides threatened to escape. Things were not perfect, but at least no one could see it. I pretended her tension didn't change the air in the room, but it did. I felt the oxygen turn sour. She scoured the shining kitchen island, still staring at Jamie.

My parents argued again that night. I knew it was about the missing pills. I was sure Jamie knew too. I thought I could hear his breath hitch and catch through the walls. Mom's voice was shaking; Dad's was slurred. They thought they were being quiet. All parents thought they could do that.

"The medicine cabinet was a mess, stuff missing, things rearranged. I know he has some pills." Mom's voice threatened to break into a shriek.

"You need to calm down. We'll send the boys out and search his room. We'll find them."

"What if he takes them?" she asked.

"He won't. He's too smart for that." Dad let out a long

sigh, and I swore the alcohol fumes floated from his mouth and into my nose again. Maybe Jamie smelled it too.

"But my oxy," Mom cut in.

"There's nothing we can do right now. We have to wait it out."

We all knew Dad wouldn't mind Jamie taking the pills. He probably pictured what it would be like to shove a handful down Jamie's throat and end it all. It was the relief he chased from the bottle. And I could almost taste the grape Advil on my lips.

"We should check the knives," Mom said. "Maybe the forks too. Oh God, what else could he have taken? What else has he stashed?"

The knife drawer had a lock on it, and I heard them jiggle it open. The clanking of silverware and the slamming of drawers came next.

"Robert?" Mom's voice shook. My stomach dropped. Jamie, who had been grunting out another series of push-ups, paused too. "We're missing a steak knife. The big one." The last bit came out a sob.

A chill raced through the house. A frigid breeze squeezed my lungs. They felt it too. Four separate bodies under one roof, each suffocating.

They marched down the hall, a united front, sort of. One soldier wobbled in his boots, the other quaked. The commotion next door would have woken me regardless. They searched his room, stripped it all. The screams of fear and rage mixed into a cocktail strong enough to rival Dad's tumblers of whiskey.

I decided to cry. I cried out my rage. I cried out frustrations, and finally, a soldier came knocking.

"Mom," I whispered. "It was me. It was me."

She gave me a blank face. I squeezed out a tear. My lip trembled. "It was me, the knife." I jumped at the sound of Jamie's door handle turning. I brought Mom to my bed and lifted the pillow. The long, serrated knife glinted in the light. It was still warm from where my head had been pressed against it.

"Why do you have this?" Mom's face was a look of anger, fear, horror, and something else.

"I was scared," I whispered. I could hear Dad talking with Jamie, keeping him in his room. Both of their words were slurred.

"You were scared?" Mom shook my shoulders. Ice crawled up my spine and broke my stare at the door, forcing me to look in her eyes.

I nodded. "After what happened last time, I just wanted it—you know, in case." Another tear fell. I let it slide down my cheek. My hand twitched, and eventually I couldn't resist and wiped it away.

She blew out her breath. She smelled like whiskey too. And lemons. She patted me on the shoulder, and I melted into her. She hugged me fiercely and whispered in my ear, "You can't be doing that. If you are scared, you need to let me know. We can get through this together."

She squeezed me again, taking the knife with her. It was shorter than I remembered. I heard the mumbled exchanges, and Jamie stepped into the hallway. He gave me a glare. I shrugged and then he did too.

The next night was Dad's turn to scream. "Honey, we have a problem."

Mom's feet pounded the floor as she raced to the kitchen. It was after dark, and I had already heard that *click* of the liquor cabinet.

"What is that? In the bottom there?"

"Powder? What is it?" Mom asked.

"I don't know, that's why I called you." Dad's voice was shaky. It was never shaky. *He* was never shaky. I wondered what it felt like to be a lion scared of a twig.

The lion stomped to Jamie's room. "What did you put in my drink? In the bottle?" I imagined him shaking Jamie by the shoulders in his bed. Jamie would have pretended to be asleep, of course. I would have too.

"I didn't do anything," Jamie said.

"Bullshit, what did you put in the whiskey?"

Mom's whispers broke the rising tension between lion and monster.

"What is it?" Dad demanded, losing the invisible thread of control.

I cracked my door. Dad's eyes were wide. Jamie's matched his look of shock.

"I can't do this anymore," Dad said.

"What is that smell?" Mom asked when she walked into the room.

I retreated to my closet. I fingered the much thinner stack of bills, just a few dollars. The biggest bill I had was a five. The feeling of letting the hundred go made my eyes well up. I had the most memories attached to that one. I stole it from my teacher's wallet during lunch.

"I asked you to check his room. What is it, Jamie? What did you do?" Dad demanded.

"I didn't do anything!"

Dad barreled past Jamie, searching his closet, under the bed. "Oh my God," Dad wailed.

A banshee screamed. It was Jamie. "I swear it wasn't me! I was going to get rid of it! I don't know how it got here!"

"Is that the stray dog? Oh my god, the cat," Mom wailed. "Not again."

"Don't come in. It's dead. I don't know for how long. It's partially skinned. Oh God." Dad wretched. "Did we interrupt your playtime with this animal? Go call the facility, honey. Now."

And then they left, leaving me alone in that house with that rotting cat. I wandered over to it, breathing in that awful scent of decaying flesh. The top half was skinned, the fur matted in dried blood. A gross piece of art fueled by pent up rage.

I found the little camera I hid on Jamie's desk, among his books he never touched. It had been pointed at his door. That camera cost me two hundred and thirty-eight dollars, and one of my favorite memories. The time I swiped a twenty from a homeless man.

I trotted down the hall, the smell of the decaying cat finally clearing from my nose. I grabbed Dad's hidden key, pulled a stool from the kitchen island, and opened the liquor cabinet. I reached around in the back, ripping the camera taped to the top. It was the hardest to hide. It cost all the jewelry I had at the pawnshop. It took me four tries to get a place to haggle with me. It was worth it. Even that pearl earring I stole from that redhead from the park was worth giving up.

I sat on Jamie's bed. It felt right to do it there, among the stinking cat and ironed curtains. I played the videos, their content sent straight to an app on my secret phone with the push of a button. I watch as crushed pills were poured and mixed into Dad's bottles. The screen was blank for a long while, Jamie entering and exiting his room. It was only activated by movement. He used to sneak out at night too. I wondered if he ever bumped into Mom or Dad. Then the cat came in, already dead and skinned, placed under Jamie's bed. There was always trouble with skinning the arms and legs.

I called the number the counselor told me to. "I have the evidence you need."

And the cops finally picked up my mother.

"Munchhausen by proxy," some social worker said. Dad didn't believe it. Of course he wouldn't. I knew he still dreamed of shoving oxycontin down Jamie's throat and ending all of the problems, as if they all stemmed from his firstborn. A sacrifice of sorts. We all knew Mom would come back home at some point, new pills in hand, the precarious veil of peace a shadow over our lives.

At least I got my brother back, for a time. My fingers burned, and I searched for an earring to steal.

COFFEE WITH THE DEVIL

I cleared my throat and wiped my palms on my pants. "I need to know. Do all of God's creatures go to heaven?"

The Devil looked back at me with his vacant eyes; they were not as terrifying as I first thought they'd be. All the scary stories in Sunday school class never mentioned how normal the Devil looked. His eyes were like dark pools of water, a mirror. Maybe that's why the emptiness of those eyes was so unsettling.

"All of God's creatures go to heaven," the Devil said. He never blinked. "Sinners and all. God loves them. He made them."

Relief flooded me—a new lightness to my body threatened to carry me away, like the steam from our cups. "Are you not a creature of God, then? Why not give up this—" I outstretched my hand and gestured around me, as if it were enough to indicate all that was wrong with this world.

He nodded slowly, his sharp nose taking a moment to inhale the coffee in front of him. It had cream in it, and I didn't know why that surprised me more than his lack of horns and tail.

"I could have gone back." He stirred the coffee. "I almost did."

I thought of a world without the Devil, without this evil and power. It was a strangely disappointing picture. No separation between the good and the terrible. There would only be the option for good. Life would be linear; we would all be equal. Maybe he was more human than I'd thought. *Or I was more devil than I'd thought.*

"But you wanted to be in control?" I asked. It's what I would have wanted.

"You could say that, but I fell into a new role when I left heaven. 'Fell from heaven,' as the poets like to call it. I created my own beings, my own devils. How could I have left them? They are not God's creatures; they are mine alone. It is because I love them that I stay. Like a father who loves his children."

"I see." I shifted in my seat, unsettled by the idea of a devil capable of love. I stood, reaching out to shake his hand.

"Where are you going?" he asked. "What makes you think you can leave?"

I slipped on my coat, ready to flee. "I'm going to tell everyone the good news, how we are all going to make it to heaven. No need to worry."

He shook his head, sipping the coffee. It was still too hot, but he swallowed anyway. "Oh no. I am afraid not. You are one of mine."

SCRIBBLES

Violet liked to read and draw; I liked to talk and walk. It had always been that way. I moved; she didn't. I was too loud; she never was.

"What are you doing, Vi?" I asked.

"Drawing our life," she said, scribbling across the page. She was on her stomach, laying on an old blanket, face scrunched in concentration. She took drawing seriously. "Pass the crayons."

I handed her the box of broken crayons and nubs of color she could barely hold. "What are you drawing?" I asked again, peeling the paper off a broken crayon. She never answered me the right way.

She huffed and held out the picture for me. The white page was full of little pencil outlines of people. The background was slowly being filled with color. Green trees, red flowers, yellow sun. She and I were next to each other, holding hands, beside to a tall person. Mom. Neither of us were colored in yet. I hoped she'd give me a purple shirt. I thought she would; twins could understand stuff like that.

I scoffed at the other two figures. "Why'd you put Donnie in there? *And* Toad?"

She snorted and went back to drawing. I sat on our island of blankets spread across the hardwood floors. The patched blankets were like our own country. We had our own rules on our land of quilts.

I watched her draw. And waited. She would answer my question, eventually. She just needed time to plan her words. She liked to read and draw. I was the one who liked to walk and talk, after all. Her words formed some order by the time the trees were colored in. She said, "Donnie and Tod, they will leave if they have to. Got to give them a chance first."

And then *Toad* walked in.

"What you brats up to?" He was older than us by four grades. He thought he was like his dad and we had to obey him too. But Donnie wasn't *our* dad, and Tod wasn't our brother, no matter what Mom said. But Mom loved Tod and Donnie. She found them somewhere, and we moved in with them. Donnie had a big house. I guess Mom liked that bit too. Mom said this was our family, and Donnie was Dad.

Our own dad was "out of the picture." I wondered if Violet could draw our own dad back in. I wonder if she remembered what he looked like. I didn't think I did, but I could make up something if she asked. I was very good at talking.

"I said, 'what are you brats up to?' Are you coloring on the floor? I'm gonna tell my dad." Tod wore a sneer;

he was excited over the prospect of getting us in trouble.

I wanted to spit on him and not care, but my stomach squeezed tight. I glanced at the paper on the ground and hoped none of the crayons made smudges on the wood when Vi colored the edges.

Toad used his foot to tap on Vi's back. "What you got there?" It was nearly a kick, but I couldn't say that, then he'd *really* show me what a kick was. Maybe bust up another one of Vi's ribs too. He picked on her more than me. She stayed still, on her stomach, but her fingers curled into her palms, unwilling to give Toad a chance to step on them.

He kicked her again, his muddy shoes leaving prints on her island of blankets. On her. *Her* space. "What is it?" he asked.

"Ribbit," she said. She didn't even look at him.

I cracked a smile.

"My name is *Tod!*" He ripped the page from her hand and studied it. "What is this?"

This time I found my voice. "It's us. And you're lucky she put you in the picture."

He scoffed and threw it on the ground. Violet's quick hand snatched it from the air as it floated down to the splintering wood floor. She pulled it to the safety of her blanket island.

"Pass me the eraser," she said.

I handed her the gummy thing, and she erased the pencil legs of Toad and blew the pieces of rubber from the page away. She shrugged and sat up. "He did this to himself."

Mom was frantic about dinner. She thought she over-cooked Donnie's steak. Toad was in a mood too, growing pains or whatever. Mom gave him some syrup, and that seemed to help. I peeked over at Vi. She stared out the window, her lips pursed. I looked at Mom; her lips were pressed together. I looked at my reflection, and my lips were closed tight too.

"Violet, Scarlett?" Mom said as she fussed over the steak. Our hotdogs were giving her no trouble.

"Yes?" I asked. Vi only looked at Mom.

"I got a call from your teacher, and some things have got to change. Scarlett, you can't just speak for your sister."

She lectured us about something. I wasn't listening. Well, sort of. I listened for the engine of Donnie's truck and the rattling of the door handle twisting.

"Do you understand?" Mom asked. "I am *not* going to repeat myself.

Vi nodded, and so did I. I hoped I agreed to something reasonable. Vi rolled her eyes and went back to staring out the window.

"She just thinks because you're twins you should at least be getting the same marks. Has no regard for how different you two are." Mom lectured the steak as if it were the teacher. But we never went to those school meetings anyway.

Toad kicked me from under the table.

"Ow!" I yelled, hoping Mom would come to my aid.

"Sorry." Toad stuck his tongue out. Mom didn't see. "Leg cramps. I was just stretching."

I was going to say something, so was Toad, Mom too, but the rattling of the doorknob made us fall quiet.

Donnie sent us to our room early. Toad too. Vi didn't get more than a bite of her hotdog. I figured it was coming, so I scarfed my down. Donnie said we were all ungrateful brats. Toad pinched us both real hard on the way to our confinements. I yelped and hollered back, but Vi just took out the eraser and took away the figure's lower half from the drawing. She took away Donnie's legs too. Now they were floating arms and bellies with heads sticking out the top. She colored me in though, and that made me feel better. She even gave me a purple shirt.

Donnie woke us up later that night, slamming the doors. He bumbled around getting to the bathroom. He was up four times, Toad too. I knew Vi was awake and could hear them, but she didn't say anything, didn't move either. She just fell back asleep, holding that eraser tight in her hand.

When Mom sported a big black eye the next morning (almost Vi's favorite shade of purple) Vi bit her lips and took out the wrinkled drawing and eraser. By now the clouds and grass were colored in, the flowers too—she used the last bit of the red crayon on those. She sat at the kitchen table with me and Donnie and stared at the man the whole time she erased his stomach and arms. Only his head floated in the picture.

He started coughing, little grunts that he usually had after smoking cigarettes. But it didn't stop. So, he went to take a nap.

Toad came into the kitchen next.

"Ribbit," I whispered when he sat in Donnie's place.

Mom smacked me on the back of the head. "Be nice."

I rubbed my skull. It stung. I think she used a spoon; I couldn't be sure. Vi rolled me the eraser from across the table and slid the picture to me. I stared at the drawing.

The trees were filled in with different greens. The sky was blue, and the sun was a perfect circle, colored yellow with orange rays bursting from the giant dot. The only blank spots were the people, except my purple shirt. Vi colored hers orange.

I looked at the eraser, the picture, then Mom. Then I looked back to Vi. She just shrugged and munched on her burned toast.

I took the gummy eraser and slid it across Mom's left leg. The pencil marks lifted, and I erased her whole left foot, careful not to smudge the crayon in the background. I passed the eraser and drawing back to Vi.

"Ah." She looked at it. "Just a little."

"Just a little," I said.

But Donnie's coughing and hacking grew worse throughout the day. Eventually, probably in a weird way to make the day end, Mom sent us to bed before dinner.

She complained of a sprained ankle and went to ice it with frozen peas.

Donnie still kept us up through the night. He hacked and hacked, coughed and coughed.

Finally, Vi said, "I think he's got to go."

I just wanted that incessant coughing to stop. I loved that word. *Incessant.* It was the perfect thing to describe the deep, wet cough that went on for hours. It was like Donnie pounded my ears with a hammer each time he coughed. Vi was right. He had to go.

"Just a little," I whispered, hoping he or Mom wouldn't hear and burst in with a wooden spoon ready to paddle our behinds.

"Just a little." Vi nodded. She took the eraser and finished erasing Donnie's floating head. I hoped Toad was next.

And the coughing stopped.

4

THIS MANY

He expected her to come walking back from the park with her feet stomping. Marching in her too-big sandals and hiking up her too-big shorts and a scowl on her cute, freckled face. But she didn't. Instead, she came running up the street and bounding up the porch stairs wearing a smile as bright as the sun.

She took big gulps from his jar of lemonade and settled in next to him in the lopsided porch swing. They watched the kids playing down the street, their laughter and screaming mixing with the summer birds chirping. There was a park at the end of the lane, and she was still catching her breath from her sprint back to the house.

"You going to go back and play?" her dad asked, worried she would notice one of her hair ribbons missing from her braids. Then he worried someone stole it, again.

"No, the birthday party is over now." She shrugged.

He was afraid to ask but did anyway. "Did you have fun? I mean, were these kids nice today?"

"Yeah! The ice cream truck came, and we each got to pick something out!"

He could see the remains of an ice cream sandwich on her lips. "It was Jenny's birthday, right?"

She nodded, hands in her pockets. She was so tiny, wearing hand-me-down clothes from her older cousin. She looked like a toddler despite being nearly seven.

"How old is Jenny now?"

"This many." She pulled her hands from her pocket and held up six fingers.

She had always been peculiar, but this made his blood freeze. Especially since he still hadn't figured out where she found them or who they belonged to.

5

THE NIGHT MAN

There were three of them, which would become a problem down the road when having to split the grim, future task. But before all of that came about, three boys managed to capture the Night Man. At least his hand. It all started in the summer, because everything good started in summer. It ended in winter, because everything sinister ended in winter.

They were busy throwing rocks into the river after church while their parents chatted and gossiped, sweat dripping down their temples, the scent of fresh-cut hay blowing around them. This was the best part of church, when the door of the stuffy sanctuary opened, and they could run down the steps and untuck their shirts and chuck rocks into the water, seeing who could make the biggest splash. The parents didn't even care, too busy finding out who the father was or why Reba left her husband.

"Where's Reggie?" Jimmy asked.

"I dunno," Lenny said, throwing a rock into the water. He dug around in his pockets. "I got some of those soda crackers from the fellowship hall when my mom was grabbing her dishes from the potluck last week, want any?" He rationed the crackers to Mike and Jimmy, giving himself a little extra.

"I heard Reggie's sick," Mike said, mouth full of cracker.

"What do you mean?" Jimmy asked, wiping crumbs from his shirt and pushing his thick glasses higher on his nose. "It's summer. Colds and flus only happen during the school year. Which is kind of convenient, if you think about it."

"That's just what I heard my mom saying," Mike said.

"I heart it was a monster that did him in," Lenny said, lowering his voice. "A monster got to him."

"Where the *hell* did you hear that?" Jimmy asked. He liked to sound tough and bold when someone was being especially ridiculous.

But Mike wondered the same thing. He also wondered what it would be like to utter the word "hell" so close to church. "Yeah, what the *hell*?" It wasn't that exciting.

"Oh, it's a monster all right." The voice came from behind them, deeper, and it made them jump and spin on their heels.

"Oh, what do you want?" Lenny asked. It was his older brother, Aaron, so he could talk to him like that.

Aaron was tall and had his keys jangling in his

pocket, the tip of a cigarette sticking out of the other pocket. He was popular and cool, a troublemaker in the sleepy town. Sometimes, late at night, you could hear him spin out, the tires of his car squealing and burning rubber as he sped through town. He pinched Lenny's cheek. "Because, baby bro, I've seen it. I've *touched* the monster."

"The monster?" Jimmy asked, all "tough guy" gone from his voice. He sounded like the real nerd he was. His nasally voice didn't help his cause. Neither did the fact that he carried a notebook and pen in his pocket.

"It is a monster," Aaron pulled out the cigarette and lit it.

The boys were transfixed with the forbidden act. They were like cats, following the glow of the lighter and embers of the cigarette with their eyes. Mike wasn't sure why he wanted to put one between his lips too.

Aaron sucked on the cigarette and looked so damn cool. He went on, "See, it's the monster trying to stop his heart." He sucked in long and slow before he blew out the smoke. A wave of the stuff washed over Lenny, and he coughed. Aaron laughed before getting serious again. "It wanders the upper side of the earth, collecting hearts for Satan. An earthside devil."

Lenny snorted. "What are you really smoking?"

Aaron stared with unblinking eyes at his little brother.

Lenny shifted on his feet. "Seriously, I'm gonna tell Mom. What you got?"

Aaron held the cigarette out to Lenny, who wrinkled

his nose. Then he held it out to Jimmy, who took an involuntary step back. Then he held it out to Mike. Mike took it in his hand, and before he had a chance to succumb to fear, he put it between his lips and took a long swallow. And coughed and coughed and coughed.

Aaron laughed. Lenny and Jimmy looked at him with a sense of awe. Worth it. *That* was why he was the leader. He did things they wouldn't. He did them poorly, but to twelve and thirteen-year-olds, doing things poorly was significantly more important than talking about doing things. Action, messy and stupid action, was always better than inaction. Mike focused on his eyes not watering and tried to ignore the burning in his throat and chest.

Arron still laughed and pulled the rest of the cigarette before stomping it out under his boot, looking back at the church. "That's what it feels like when the Night Man comes for you."

"What the hell are you talking about?" Lenny asked, trying to get back some authority he'd lost when he snubbed the cigarette.

Aaron smacked Lenny's head. "Don't let Mama catch you using that language."

Lenny rubbed his head. Jimmy, the scholar wannabe, finally piped up. "But who is the Night Man, and what about hearts?"

Aaron smiled a wide grin. "The Night Man. He once was an angel—"

"So was Satan," Jimmy said.

"Do you wanna know or what?" Aaron snapped.

The boys nodded.

"What happened to Reggie?" Mike asked.

"What *almost* happened to me. And you all." Aaron pulled another cigarette out but didn't light it. "The Night Man belongs to Satan now. Some say he was tricked by Satan into joining him. But the Night Man wanted to go back to wherever—heaven or the celestial realm or wherever those things live. But Satan wouldn't let him. Not until he provided Satan and his devils with a hundred thousand frozen hearts. The hearts are like souls, only better, and harder to get. So that's what the Night Man does. He comes at night and reaches into the chests of little children and plucks out their hearts. They don't recover. They die in the hospital with names like pneumonia or colic. He preys on the weak ones, trying to collect as many hearts as he can. The little ones are easier." He jabbed Jimmy in the side and made him jump. "They don't squirm as much."

"You're full of shit," Lenny laughed.

"Am I?" Aaron asked, eyebrows raised. "I've felt him reach inside my bones and try and wiggle my heart loose. Are you sure he hasn't tried to go after your heart?" He pointed to Mike. "Just ask your pal Mikey here, he'll tell you."

"Well, Mike?" Jimmy asked.

Lenny crossed his hands over his chest and tried to look big. He always tried to look big when Aaron was around.

Mike nodded. "Yeah, I felt him once. And I'm pretty sure he's after my little brother."

Mike thought his little brother would get stronger. But he didn't. Little Andy grew pale and thin despite the summer sun and fresh air. When fall came, he began to look more like the skeletons decorating the yards.

"The doctors don't know why he's been feeling so poorly," Mike's mom said into the phone. "Yeah, they think he will outgrow it. They said he probably needed more milk in his diet. Takes after his father I guess, weak stomach."

Milk wouldn't do shit. Andy woke each night, screaming and yelping and tearing at his chest. His skin was always so cold.

Mike took to sleeping less. Forcing himself awake and forcing himself to peer down from the top bunk to make sure no figure (other than his own) lingered over Andy. Mike caught him once. The Night Man. He had his hand clear in Andy's chest, and Mike was sure the monster would have pulled little Andy's heart loose if

Mike hadn't yelled out, jumping down from the top of the bunk bed and making a loud *crash*.

Mom and Dad said he needed to act like the big kid. Nightmares were just for little kids. The walking nightmare wandered the streets at night, through walls, and through skin.

"We gotta stop him," Mike said at the church harvest party. "The Night Man won't give up on Andy. It's only a matter of time now."

"I don't think this is real," Jimmy said, stuffing his mouth with a caramel apple.

Lenny talked through a mouthful of popcorn. "I don't know. Aaron hasn't told me the joke is up. And he usually does when I pester him enough. And trust me, I've been pestering. And Reggie..."

Reggie died that summer, infection in his lung or something.

"So, what are you gonna do?" Jimmy asked, rubbing a smudge from his glasses.

"We are gonna catch the Night Man." And Mike suddenly craved a cigarette and smoke in his lungs.

"Do we have to do this?" Jimmy asked from his spot on the closet floor. He pushed the glasses up on his nose with a quivering hand.

"Of course we do," Mike said. His voice wobbled, but his resolve held firm.

"Yeah," said Lenny from his place under the bed. He

pushed his baseball cap farther on his head, swatting dust bunnies away. "We gotta do it. You're not gonna chicken out now, tough guy?"

"It's not my brother," Jimmy mumbled. He sank back into the shadows of the closet, clutching the flashlight with both hands like a weapon.

"No, it isn't." Mike gripped his own flashlight tight in his hand, an ax in the other. He pointed it at Jimmy. "But when he gets Andy, then what? He'll come after *you*. You're probably the next smallest one here. Weak too. You *always* get a cold. You probably have one starting now. Then it'll be Lenny and me after that."

Jimmy swallowed hard and nodded.

"You know what to do?" Mike asked.

Jimmy nodded, clicked on the flashlight, and shined it on the silent little boy sitting in bed watching the older boys squabble. Little Andy had dark eyes and swallowed down a yawn.

"And you?" Mike pointed to Lenny, covered in dust he kicked loose under the bed. Lenny nodded and tapped the baseball bat at his side

Mike swallowed hard and nodded to his brother. "Now, don't tell Mom what we are doing, okay, Andy? It's real important she don't know."

Andy nodded and settled under his blankets, trying to get warm before the cold came. The cold always came.

Mike hung back in the shadows. He needed to stand. Sitting would mean falling asleep, and that would mean him. Then the Night Man would push his bony fingers between the child's ribs and take hold of the beating heart. The Nightman would hold Andy's heart until it froze, another one collected to pay off his debt.

But now I'm here, Mike thought. The hours ticked on.

The cold seeped through the walls, Mike thought he felt the Night Man's exhale. The Night Man had come for him once. He had woken to find the finger stuck in his chest, for only a moment, before the Night Man pulled his hand from his ribs and fled. Sometimes he woke to a cold ache in his chest, and he was left wondering if he'd escaped death once more.

He'd felt the Night Man's presence more than once—which is why he recognized him when the monster crept through the window. The Night Man leaned over the bed where Andy slept, a thin, grey arm poised over the little boy's ribs.

Now, Mike thought—willing Jimmy to grow a pair and shine the light. *Do it now.*

The Night Man withdrew a hand from his cloak, and his long fingers hovered over Andy. *Now!* Mike screamed in his mind. The Night Man's icy fingers plunged into Andy's chest and slipped through his ribs. As Mike let out a scream, Jimmy's light shone from the closet.

The Night Man paused for only a moment—but it was enough. Mike used light as his target, and he slashed the arm where it rested with that blunt ax he had stolen from the woodpile out back. And the Night Man howled like a banshee and fled.

The severed hand rested on Andy. Mike took the thing, it didn't even bleed, and hurled it to the ground. It was like a block of ice.

"Yuck!" Lenny said, crawling awkwardly from under the bed, giving the hand a wide berth.

"Where were you?" Mike hissed.

"Fell asleep." Lenny shrugged.

"You idiot—"

"Is it gone?" Andy asked from his little nest in bed.

"We got 'em," Mike said, a big smile on his face.

The boys tore into the night—racing through the corn-fields and howling at the moon.

"What should we do with it?" Jimmy asked, pointing to the shoe box containing the Night Man's hand.

"We burn it!" Lenny said, drunk on victory. "What better way to get rid of ice than with fire?"

"Burn it with what?" Jimmy asked.

Lenny smiled. "With fire."

"Well, no shit," Mike said. The idea was sounding better. The shoebox in his hands grew colder by the minute.

"I know a spot," Lenny said, and after more whoops and hollers they found themselves on a dead-end road, gravel and leaves crunching under their feet.

"Where'd you get the lighter?" Jimmy asked.

Lenny shrugged. "Aaron."

At times, Lenny's memory of events and what *actually* happened intertwined with the stories of his older brother, creating a fast-paced and adventurous life of his own. But Lenny had never smoked a cigarette. He'd never stolen a candy from the drug store. But sometimes he forgot that he was boring and used his cool older brother as a smokescreen.

Jimmy kicked the gravel flat, and Mike placed that cardboard box on the ground.

"Do you want to do it?" Lenny held the lighter out to Mike, his brother's mischievous energy and bravery gone.

Mike cleared his throat. *No,* he thought. "Yes," he said.

He settled next to the shoe box, not daring to open it again. Instead, he set the corner on fire. It took a few tries (he had never used a lighter) and the trio had to stand close to block the wind, but it eventually lit. And it burned. And somewhere deep in the woods, a scream of the Night Man made the birds scatter.

Mike laughed nervously. Lenny did too. Jimmy stared wide-eyed into the forest.

"Hey," Lenny said. "Want one?" He held up three cigarettes.

"Aaron's gonna kill you," Mike said, a smile creeping onto his face.

Lenny shrugged again. "At least we got the Night Man."

"Mike," Lenny whispered from the pew behind him at church. "I don't know what to do." Lenny's eyes were craters in his head, dark circles framing them.

"Later," Mike whispered, chewing his lip all through the hallelujahs and hymns.

Jimmy jumped every time the organ started, his eyes never still.

The trio met at the same spot they had that summer, after the hymns were sung and the mothers gathered, anxious for their vice. Gossip. Some stole a smoke, maybe a sip out of the little flask hidden in the glove compartment of the truck.

The wind howled, and it looked like rain. The frozen river was gnarled and cracked, much like the Night Man's hands. The vices would be cut short today, which was a shame. Indulging in vices didn't count at church.

"I don't know what to do—" Lenny's eyes darted about. "I hear him all the time—I *feel* him. I can't explain it."

"We have to fix this," Mike said.

"How?" Jimmy asked. "What can we do?"

They met at the same place they burned the hand. Their desperation for an answer made them bold. Even Jimmy didn't question Mike when it was suggested they sneak out as soon as it got dark.

"It's like he follows me," Jimmy said, his usual slight frame even more narrow. The wind could have blown him away if it tried hard enough. "I'm cold, all the time. So cold. I'm never warm."

"I'm always tired."

"I'm always hungry. Thirsty."

"I'm always afraid."

Mike understood it all too well. The cold of the night had settled in his bones and never left. The hunger in his body only grew fiercer. Food turned to ice in his mouth. But Andy was okay.

"What do we do?" Lenny asked.

Mike swallowed hard. "We ask the Night Man."

"What?" Jimmy's eyes scanned the gravel road, only illuminated by the light of the moon. It's like the stars were hiding from them.

Mike swore he could still smell the ash of the burning box and hand.

"Why would he be here?" Jimmy asked.

"Because I am always with you." The voice came from all around them. A man appeared from the fog, his cloak whipping in the wind. He only had one hand.

"Why are you doing this?" Mike asked. Any fear he had was replaced by his hunger for an answer.

"You stole from me, and now I am stuck here, unable to leave or collect my hearts and souls. I may as well make you feel like I do. Trapped in an endless world with only a growing emptiness."

"I want this to end," Mike said.

"Then give me my hand."

The eyes of the trio wandered to the spot where the hand once burned.

"We can't," Mike said.

"Then replace what you have stolen."

A *thud* made the boys jump, and on the ground between the three of them was an ax.

6

CROWS

She covered her mouth when she spoke, at least when she was outside. But she had been known to cover her smiles and mouth when near windows too. A strange habit she started as a child, and it was only stranger as she grew.

She covered her body with thick sweaters and denim. Mittens even in summer. "To keep the birds from splitting my skin," she explained.

"They won't get you." Cam rolled his eyes. Older brothers always did that though. He pinched her, but it didn't hurt. The thick coat was enough armor this time.

"They'll get my tongue," she said, her tongue hidden behind her hands. "It's like a worm to them, ripe for the picking."

"No, they won't." Cam stuck his tongue out and wiggled it. The pink thing tempted the birds. "See?"

"Stop it," she said. "Put that thing back in your face."

"I can't hear you when you cover your mouth like that."

She ignored him. He loved to taunt her. But she loved her tongue attached to her mouth better.

"Grandma says crows know where their friends have died, and they won't come back to that spot, kinda like how we don't go to the cemeteries because it's creepy."

"Grandma also says flamingos are pink." She picked up a sick with her free hand and hit a tree trunk too. The *crack* spread through the forest, and she hoped it would make the birds flee.

"They are!" he cried, throwing a rock into a pile of dry and crunchy autumn leaves.

"I don't think so," she said.

"It's 'cause of what they eat."

Like pink tongues? "Okay, so what if she's right about the crows?" she asked.

"Well," he threw another rock into the trees, "what if I make a safe space for you?" He held the rock like a weapon, and she took a step back.

"What do you mean?"

He chucked the rock at the tree. "I'll find a crow, put it down." He fiddled with the rock in his hand, trying to find the best way to hold it. "Then we make all the other crows see the dead one. Then they never come back. A crow graveyard they'll never visit. You're safe."

"No," she said, her palm flat against her lips. "No." She ran inside, the only thing worse than a lone crow was a mob of angry crows.

"What's got you all twisted?" her grandma asked as she tore inside, slamming the screen door behind her.

She wanted to lock the door, but her granny would make a bigger scene.

"It's Cam," she explained. "He's gonna kill a crow to make a safe space. A place I can go where the crows won't bother me." She had a hand covering her mouth. She was by a window after all. A screen was no barrier to those razor-sharp beaks.

"Makes sense," Grandma said. The old woman stood looking out the window and watched Cam throw rocks at the surrounding trees in the yard. She wiped her hands on her apron and faced the girl. "Crows are also an omen. They are thought to bring change, so maybe it would be best to embrace them. They have the gift of foresight after all."

Grandma is losing it.

"Well?" Grandma asked, wiping her hands on her apron. "What are you gonna do? Go back out there and show the birds what's what? Or show Cam what's what?"

The girl went outside, leaving Grandma in the kitchen, muttering things about omens and flamingos. She scanned the tree line and found Cam hunkered at the base of a tree trunk.

"Ready?" Cam whispered in her ear, pulling her close.

"What?" she whispered. It was the natural thing to do, when someone whispered it was rude not to whisper back.

"See those two?" he pointed to the two crows resting on a branch.

Her blood ran cold, like a river freezing in her body, holding her in place. She pulled her thick coat close around her neck. "No, don't," she said, pulling Cam's hand.

"What?" He pinched her arm, hard. It stung through the coat. "Kill a crow, get a safe spot. Simple."

"But Grandma said they have the gift of foresight."

"What the hell is that?" He lifted his hand, cocked his arm back, and let the rock fly. And one of the crows fell. The other flew away. A small *thud* hit the dirt.

Cam ran to it, picked it up by its wing, and searched the trees for the second crow. "See, the other one is gone. It's true, they won't come back."

The girl didn't feel much better, but she slowly lowered her hand from her mouth, leaving her lips and tongue exposed. She muttered something about foresight, which apparently crows had. But if she'd had that gift, she might have seen the crow waiting in a tree. She might have known she needed to have her eyes closed tight. But she didn't have the gift of foresight, and never would, because the black bird swooped down and plucked out her eyes.

7

SALAMANDERS

"Well, hello there, Miss Missy," Gunner called from across the lot.

Missy's head snapped up and searched for the origin of that long drawl, but she knew the voice's owner long before her eyes fell on the shaggy, brown hair of Gunnar Gibbs. She nodded, hoping it would be enough, but he shuffled over, his boots scraping across the hot asphalt.

"What have you got going on here?" he asked, watching the young high school kid load her truck with fifty-pound bags of feed. Mostly grain for the horses, a few packages of feed for the chickens.

The sun was nearing its high point in the sky, and she thanked the young kid working, begging him with her eyes not to go back into the store. He left anyway. She chalked it up to his youth and inexperience. It was unreasonable to hope that a sixteen-year-old farm kid would be able to read the signs of a woman in distress.

"Hi there, Gunnar," she said, a polite smile on her

face. She didn't know what else to do with it. *Do I know how to scowl?* She clutched the keys in her hand, hoping she'd manage a good grip if she needed to aim for an eye.

"What have you going on here?" he asked again, hands on her truck. It was like his hands were on her skin, and her stomach rolled.

"Just some feed. Normally I have enough to last a few months, but the old lady is struggling to keep weight on." She thought of the mare. Her old teeth made it hard for her to chew the hay and grass these days. She'd been eating double, sometimes triple, the amount of grain just to help avoid her ribs poking through. That old horse was also the only thing pulling her out of bed these past few months.

Missy hopped in her truck, hoping he'd release his hold on the truck bed so she could be on her way.

He kept a hand on the truck and made his way to the driver's side, tracing his hand over the door. He leaned in through her open window. "Gonna be a lot for you to unload this yourself since the mister passed and all."

"I'll manage." She tried to start the truck, but her hands fumbled, and she dropped the keys.

"Such a shame." He shook his head. The smell of vanilla tobacco from his lips filled her nose. It was the same brand Lucas used to smoke.

"Thank you for your condolences," she cleared her throat, "but I'm just fine."

His hand gripped the truck's door, fingers sliding into the cab. "Such a shame. Strange that not one, but two, salamanders made their way into the lemonade. Was it only months ago? At the church potluck?"

Missy swallowed hard. *He was there. He knows.*

"Miss Missy—"

"Mrs.," she corrected.

"If that's what you like. What is the title for young, pretty widows like yourself?"

She found her resolve and started the old engine. She said a silent prayer in her head, willing the old beat-up truck to make it the winding drive back to her home. This was her husband's truck—*late* husband. Why late? Was it some sort of poetic prose people used, believing deep down they'd come back, they were simply running a little late? Lucas was always late.

The truck still smelled of him at times. She'd get just a whiff of that vanilla tobacco, and it gave her a moment's smile. She smelled it now, coming off of Gunnar, and her stomach soured.

She looked at his hands still gripping her door, his dirty finger sliding into her space. "It's Mrs."

"I'll follow you back, make sure you don't break your back unloading those bags."

She should have said something, gotten out and told him what's what, made a scene in this public place full of witnesses. But she didn't. Instead, she just drove home.

She chewed on her lip, her gut told her this day would come, the way he would look at her. The way he let his hand linger too long on her arm as he passed by, the way he would squeeze behind her in a crowded space. He would press his body against hers just for a moment.

Gunnar's truck followed close behind her. He looked like he was in no hurry at all. He smoked a cigarette, and when she occasionally cast a glance in her rearview mirror, he would smile and wave.

When she reached her long gravel driveway, she slowed to a crawl, prolonging the interaction. Eventually, time caught up with her, and she parked the truck near the small barn. The two horses bickered but stopped their foolishness when she stepped out. They trotted over, hoping for some treat. She walked over to the gate and patted them on the nose, but they lost interest when they discovered she had no carrots or sugar cubes hidden in her pockets. They went back to grazing and bickering. She tried to ignore the door slam of Gunnar's truck, but it made her flinch.

She felt him come up behind her, a weight pressing against her backside despite him still being several feet away. She turned, determined to have an air of authority. "You can put them right in there." She pointed to the open barn door.

The sun beat down on the pair, but Gunnar smiled despite the sweat and heat, lobbing the heavy bags over his shoulders and carrying them to the barn. He was done in only a few trips, and she stumbled over her thanks.

"Anytime, Missy. Despite this being a small town, we like to take care of our own. If there is anything you need during this trying time for you, you just let me know."

Missy nodded. "I appreciate that." For a moment, she thought it would be over.

He took the end of his shirt and wiped the sweat from his brow. "It sure is a scorcher today. I would sure be obliged for some of your famous lemonade."

"Have none," she snapped.

"Ah." He gave her a slow smile. "Makes sense, after all, you know... But you could make some."

"I have some sweet tea," she admitted, already walking toward the small house.

"That's mighty fine." His smile was the same one he wore at the church potluck. A hyena's grin. He was rarely there, at church, but he occasionally came with his mama to the picnics and harvest festivals, gabbing with the other boys in town about his work or prospect of new work.

He lingered over the food, eating triple helpings from Missy's casserole, hovering near her and the other ladies. He got drunk off the punch but stared unblinking as her Lucas drank the lemonade.

"It was a miracle that newt didn't make its way into the pitcher, only the glass," the preacher's wife had commented.

Others had nodded. Two salamanders dancing in a pool of lemonade in the bottom of a dead man's solo cup. *Lucas's cup.*

"One of those critters could've gotten into the soup, maybe even the salads," others had exclaimed.

Gunnar followed her close then, and he followed her close now. She thought she could feel his hand reach out to tug on her hair. She forced the goosebumps to flee. It was sweltering, but they stayed prominent and bumpy on her skin. *Just like a rough-skinned newt.*

She stomped the dust from her shoes on the porch and marched in, Gunnar close behind. She didn't flinch when the deadbolt give its signature *click.*

"Have a seat there." She pointed to the table.

He did, leaning on the back two legs of the chair. For a moment he looked as if he were going to put his dirty boots on the table, like he was making this his own space.

"I figured you'd drop by, so I made it sweeter than normal. You prefer things on the sweeter end, right?" She poured a large glass of the sweet tea from a cold pitcher.

"That's right." He licked his lips.

She handed him the glass, ignoring his dirty fingers rubbing against hers. She watched him take four long swigs. Some dribbled down his chin.

She couldn't bite her words back. "I know what you did, Gunnar. I know it was you who put those newts in the lemonade. Why? Why would you do that?" Her voice wobbled, and bile crept up her throat.

Gunnar chuckled. "That sounds crazy, Miss Missy." His eyes darkened, and the hyena's smiled disappeared, leaving only a row of teeth. "I would be careful who you would be spreadin' that story to."

"I know what you did to the lemonade." There wasn't a shake in her voice.

He laughed and licked his lips. "You know? I wasn't really in the mood for lemonade anyway. And this is finer than any lemonade you made for any potluck." He grinned, reaching out to touch her bare arm. "What did you put in this?"

"It's just black tea that's been steeping in my fridge for two days." She pulled away, looking at the locked door. "Along with an unholy amount of sugar. And not one, not two, but *three* salamanders."

8

FRESH INK

The bell chimed as I walked through the familiar doors. The scent of ink and blood filled my lungs. I stretched them in and out as I breathed in deep, finally getting a feel for them. I was sure I saw the particles floating in the air as I sucked them down. I walked to the counter where a bald-headed man asked for my name.

"Legion," I said.

His eyebrows rose. His tattooed arms pointed to the back booth. I walked the familiar path.

"Same thing, same place?" her burgundy lips asked.

We both knew what I wanted. It was just a strange formality she must keep up, a way of asking "this again?" but more polite.

I took my usual seat, stretching my hand open and closed. I didn't bother asking how she knew it was me; she just did. Maybe this was something she did for the others. Maybe there were more of me walking earthside than I'd thought.

The familiar buzz of the machine reached my ears. She didn't need to sketch out the art anymore. It was probably like a signature to her now, repeating the same image over and over and over.

The needle pierced the flesh and injected blue and black ink, a constant song of skin splitting and tearing.

My free arm wandered. I let my fingertips trace over this new face. It was cold. I rolled my tongue over the teeth, slicing it against the sharp points. I didn't feel the warmth of blood or taste the iron. I didn't feel anything. The needle continued to tear at the skin.

"You *still* don't bleed, man," she said, holding the buzzing machine in her hands.

I yearned for some adrenaline to surge this body and push blood through these empty veins. I wanted it to pound in my chest and pulse in my ears. I needed it to drown out all the noise. A faint outline of a tree emerged from the ink. A lone pine tree. I could have had a forest by now. If they were on the same body, that is. She had tattooed dozens.

"Think you'll keep this one?" She knew I wouldn't.

I shrugged. The once unblemished skin was a smattering of blue ink on the cream canvas. I'd come back for another. On a fresh arm. But maybe she was right, maybe this could be the body for me. The more I wore it, the more it grew on me. This one had very pleasant skin.

9

A HOUSE BY THE SEA

THE WOMAN

I never thought funerals could be so cheerful, but there I was, surrounded by the people I loved and the scent of fresh tulips permeating the air. Orange tulips. Everyone must have known those were my favorite. The tables were full of them, gifts from thoughtful friends.

It seemed odd at first, a reception after the service, but as I lifted the fork full of cheesecake into my mouth, I couldn't disagree with the practicality. What better way to replenish your strength after standing for hours, watching a coffin lower to the ground, than standing around some more to hear the sniffles and eat your fill of cheesecake?

I couldn't wait to get out of this place and forget the faces of pity everyone shot at me. But I couldn't blame them; I gave my kids the same look.

Erin, my friend of twenty years, stopped my search for more cake. Chocolates would do, and I popped a few from my pocket into my mouth.

"So, you still going to go through with it?" she asked.

I had my speech prepared. "Yes," I said. "You should really see it. It's just something else."

"But you're fixing it up all on your own?"

"Mostly cosmetic stuff, but yes. Jerry said the foundation was firm and the walls were good, so nothing to worry about but paint and flooring and the fun stuff." I felt myself start to ramble.

"I'm sorry you have to do it alone."

"I don't *have* to do it. I want to. I think time away from—" I lost the word, so I just gestured around me, and she nodded. "I just need time," I finished. *An ocean of time.*

She looked at me with furrowed eyebrows and pursed lips, like when she looked at her misbehaving grandchildren. I looked to my own kids corralling *their* own kids. The eldest grandchild was only ten, but she looked like she was a hundred with that mopey face she wore, her nose buried in a book. I envied her escape. The other kids were playing tag in the grass, trying not to think about their sad parents. They couldn't be sad. I didn't blame them. They barely knew Jerry. Christmas cards and the occasional phone call just weren't enough to connect. He was only an idea to them.

They will act like this at my funeral. Whenever that would be. Maybe not running around, but just as distant and detached. Distracted. My own kids looked miserable. I could almost see the heat radiate from their aching joints, a consequence of a rushed economy flight across the sea.

This was an inconvenience. Their childhood home was no longer available for them to use as a place to land either. I would have been frustrated too. But wasn't death always inconvenient? The wind blew my hair into my face, and I batted it away.

It took me a few moments to realize Erin was still in front of me nodding. What else was there to say?

I stared at Erin's wrinkled hands. I wanted those hands. I wanted the years of something other than my hometown blemishes on my skin. She had scars, her veins were rivers, the wrinkles were maps to the places and the things she'd done. My hands were wrinkled and pale, but not nearly as haggard and beautiful.

When things finally died down and the last of the goodbyes were said, I began organizing the tulips in the backseat of our car. *My* car, exclusively, now, I suppose. It felt rather odd to have shared your life with someone for forty years and then suddenly revert from the "we" to "I."

But we try. I try.

"Mom, are you serious about this?"

"Good grief, Auggie." I said it with a smile, but he still looked at me with a flat face. He wasn't himself. He was puffier than I remembered, like a statue in a wax museum. He had a vague piece of my son to him, but he was different now.

"I just don't know why you guys couldn't have stayed here."

"We retired," I sighed. "And we wanted a project.

Neither of us wanted to sit in front of the telly and get soft. We thought this was a good project. It *is* a good project. You should really see it."

"I know, I know, a beautiful cottage right on the sea with a cute little path and a big yard."

"What's not to love?"

"I don't know," he snapped. "The shag carpet, yellow wallpaper, and cracked floors?"

"We were going to fix it together," I said.

"And now you're alone, so find a place here, with your friends." Auggie stole a glance at his sister, June. "She is worried about you, we all are, but we won't be here to take care of you."

"That has never been an issue."

He looked like he was going to say something. His lips pursed and jaw tightened. He looked so much like my Jerry, but he relaxed when June Bug joined us.

"Hey Mom." She glanced at Auggie, who shook his head imperceptibly, at least he thought so. I raised my brows at the two.

"What?" June started. "We are just worried. Do you even know the first thing about flipping a house?"

I threw up my hands. "The bones are fine. That's what your dad said! The foundation and walls are fine. I can't do any damage other than cosmetic! And trust me, anything I do will be an improvement."

"Fine, fine. I just—I don't know! You're edging closer to seventy than sixty and—"

"You're worried about *me*?" I couldn't help but grin. "What? That I may fall and break my legs? The same two legs that carried me across not one but *two* marathons last year?"

June held up her hands in defense. "All right, all right, I just had to—you know, be the concerned daughter." There was an awkward silence before she added with a sly smile, "You guys would have killed each other working on this."

Auggie smiled a real smile, not even a hint of guilt for doing it at a funeral.

"Yeah, we would have." I laughed, and that might have been the last time I laughed. "But he had agreed to let me do what I wanted to the house so long as he got to do whatever he wanted to the workshop."

"Ma, why'd you have to sell the house?" Auggie finally asked.

"Because we wanted this new one."

"It was paid off!"

"So is this one." I smiled calmly, and I saw them shift, not wanting to rock the boat. I didn't have the heart to tell them the boat crashed along the rocks, and I was hanging onto splinters. And this old house.

The birds scattered, and the kids wrestling paused to watch their wings stretch.

"Look," Auggie said. "We just want you to, you know, not be alone during this time."

I thought about scaring him, taking it as an invitation to join him in Germany, but he sensed this opening and quickly followed up with, "You have friends here, a life."

"A life with your dad. I want to finish the new life we planned. Just relax, okay?"

He sighed, and June nodded. We hugged and kissed and said goodbye. I squeezed them fiercely. It had been —what? Four years since they made it back to the states. I doubted I'd see them for another four. Their spouses would collect the kids, and they'd head off to the airport together, one to Germany, serving in the army, and one to France, also for work.

"It'll be okay," I reassured them from the rearview mirror as I lost them around the bend. I knew this was more for me than anyone else though. I couldn't help but glance down at my hand to see if any scars or rivers appeared.

I finally saw the house after weaving between the potholes of the long driveway. The storage container with all of our things was nestled against the house. We had planned on living minimally while we replaced the floor. "No sense moving everything twice," Jerry had said, and I couldn't have agreed more. Except I was pulling out a sleeping bag and air mattress from my trunk, and I couldn't help but think of the comfortable mattress buried in the container among our other junk.

The house was a glorified shack with weathered and splintering walls, the wrap-around porch bending in some places. But still, the house stood tall, even among the taller trees. The ocean's roar greeted my ears. The salt filled my lungs. I smiled despite the chill seeping into my bones, turning my joints to ice.

Entering the house did nothing to suppress the

wind. The carpet sank under my feet, and I swore plumes of dust rose with each step, swirling with the breeze that managed to seep through the walls. The house was empty save for an old refrigerator, clawfoot bathtub, a dated chandelier, and an old wingback chair positioned in the center of the open living room.

Dust floated down from the ceiling and settled among the grime on the floor. I eyed the chandelier. "We're home, Jer bear."

He'd fallen in love with that ugly light fixture, and now that he was gone, I should have had no qualms about changing it, but I found I rather liked the crooked and ugly piece above the living room now.

I found the master room, well, the biggest room. The portable fan on the queen-sized mattress hummed and shook more dust loose. As I inflated the mattress, I did a rapid and surface-level clean and felt better about everything, like I was wiping the grime from today away too.

The sun was still high in the sky, only obscured by the clouds. I spent the rest of the afternoon unpacking the flowers and my suitcase. I couldn't help but stare out the windows each time I passed one, each angle from the house a new view to treasure. A wooded area on one side, a straight line to the coast on the other. It was a dream. The constant crashing of waves was a metronome I worked to. The waves were like a drum that beat my bones and shook my core. I looked at my hands again, still pale and wrinkled.

I pulled back my hair and tied it in a low bun and set my sights on the bathroom. I unloaded the supplies I had thought to bring with me from when we first dropped off the pod, what, three weeks ago? Was it only three weeks since we bought this place, packed up our old house, and moved things? Then the death, funeral, memorial, and now this?

I scrubbed the yellowing vanity and toilet. I was still in my funeral uniform, but I didn't care about the bleach straining my black dress. I even got on my hands and knees to scrub around that clawfoot tub. A little ember of excitement ignited in me when I imagined the long bubble baths I'd enjoy here, the ocean view just out the window, framed by towering trees.

I thought it was a good idea, back when I had ideas.

I had to take a walk outside, around on the porch. I breathed in the clean air and let the salt wash the bleach from my sinuses. I forgot to eat dinner. Instead, I found myself nestled in my makeshift bed with a sleeping bag and flat pillow and couldn't be bothered to get up. I stared out the window at the graying sky, still wearing that damned funeral dress. I told myself I'd cut it into rags. I fell asleep before I could catch the shadows slipping inside the walls.

At least that's how I remembered it all starting.

THE GHOST

She didn't hear me settle into the corners of the room and melt into the walls. She slept fitfully. She tossed and turned in rhythm with the waves. But she woke and convinced herself she slept well. Good for her. She had been telling herself that each morning she woke here. I didn't know how long it had been. I didn't deal with time.

I followed close behind as she trotted down the creaking stairs. She said hello to the chandelier, like she did every morning, and made herself a pot of coffee. The kitchen looked more like a kitchen since her recent trip to the grocery store. She forgot coffee again, so she was stuck reusing the old grounds. This was what—day three of that?

She murmured to herself, "807 Friends Way, Rock-away City," forcing a smile on her face each time she repeated it. She hadn't had to memorize an address for thirty-eight years, and the new incantation messed with her mind. Well, it was one of the several things pulling at the folds of her brain. I was one of them, of course.

She poured more milk than coffee into her mug, and she surveyed the room. The carpet was gone, torn to pieces and in the dumpster out back. It left exposed hardwood flooring in such terrible shape she bumped up "replace flooring" to her next thing on her list.

She stared at the chandelier from her spot in the wingback chair. "Looks good, Jerry."

"It does," I said.

She heard me, of course she did. If she looked closely, she could have seen my breath turn the dust around her. But she nodded and closed her eyes while she took a gulp of the warm coffee and pretended not to hear me. The weak coffee ran down her throat. Some dribbled from her lip.

She worked through the morning, cleaning and wiping down the splintering floors. Measuring and re-measuring the living room and kitchen. She swept and mopped again. She imagined she could still smell the tulips, now dried out and crumbling on the kitchen counters.

"Go outside," I whispered.

She did as I told her and walked into the fresh air, though she didn't know it was me who commanded her. She liked to think she had her own ideas. Everyone liked to think that.

Her lungs hummed as they emptied of dust and filled with salt. She licked her lips. She walked the trail that led to the beach; I trailed in her footsteps. We reached the clearing between the trees. She sat on the bench that overlooked the waves, among the tall grass and the purple wildflowers.

She was angry, her hands flexed into fists. Her eyes scanned the trail, looking for a rock, stick, anything to throw into the water below. The lookout was the perfect place for launching anger and frustration and fear. And memories. She stared at her hands and stood, walking back the way we'd come.

I missed my chance, but I knew there would be more.

We made our way back down the trail, past the sea, and back to the house. I let her feel my whispers against her neck each step we took back.

"Oh Jerry, what am I doing here?" she asked the chandelier.

Her phone rang, and she searched for it, finding it

wedged in that old wingback chair. I think it was green once. It's was gray now.

"Hello?" she answered.

"Hey Mom," June said.

"Hey sweetheart, what's going on? How are the classes going?"

The smile split her face and filled the room with more brightness than the chandelier. I shrank back into the walls.

"Classes are fine. My students are much more motivated when finals are just around the corner. Hey, I was just wondering, why you didn't call Auggie yesterday? For his birthday? He called me and said he couldn't get a hold of you."

The woman glanced at the wall next to the fridge where the calendar was. Where it *should* have been. At least that's where she kept it at the old house. She ran her hand through her silver hair, getting her fingers tangled in her bun.

"Oh yeah, I was just going to call him. I lost my phone for a bit there. Your call helped me find it actually."

"He said he called three times."

"I couldn't find my phone. I love you, sweetie, but I'm going to call him now."

"Wait—before you go, what's the new address? I want to send you something." We both heard the smile in her voice.

"Oh, 1411, North Main Street."

"That's the old place," June laughed into the phone. "I need the new place."

"Right." The woman chuckled, still trying to get her fingers and ring untangled from her hair. "Old habits. It feels strange to say something new after all these years. It's—" She glanced at the note taped to the refrigerator. "807 Friends Way, Rockaway."

"Thanks, tell Auggie I say hi." And June hung up.

The woman paced across the creaking and splintering wood floors. She stopped at the wall and picked at the wallpaper, peeling back the layers. It was like peeling her own skin, and she stared at her hands again. *Still no scars,* she thought.

She eventually pulled out her phone and checked her calendar before giving Auggie a call and the same excuse about losing her phone. They chatted about nothing in particular; she peeled the wallpaper the whole time.

She got off the phone—still apologizing to Auggie for misplacing her cellphone, but never once about maybe, potentially, probably forgetting his birthday. She looked at her hands and back at the walls and peeled some more.

I had her right where she needed to be.

THE WOMAN

I started my day like normal. I walked down the creaking and cold stairs, said hello to Jerry, a peculiar habit I'd picked up and refused to quit. I sometimes heard him whisper back. I knew it was all in my head, but part of me thought he lingered here. I listened for him, hoping he'd help me pick out colors and tile and backsplashes like he said he would.

I made some weak coffee in the pot I found at the thrift store. I sipped the weak stuff as I walked around the cold room. The creaking of the floorboards under my toes made me feel like I wasn't alone.

Things had been so strange these past few months. I knew after a life surrounded by routine and people it would be a change, but nothing prepared me for the strange noises at night. I always woke with a dull headache. It could be the mattress. But things moved. I lost my calendar, and it hung from the refrigerator, like it had always done. Then one day it was gone. I felt like I was being watched. My chocolates were gone. I always had some in my pockets but someone was stealing them. Sometimes I had to fight the urge to sprint as fast as my old bones would let me back into the house after my afternoon walks. My heart thumped in my chest, like someone was chasing me all the time.

I stared at the now clean wall. The stripping of the wallpaper took longer than expected. There were layers upon layers of the stuff. I watched the decades go by in the shape of wallpapers—peachy floral print for the nineties, baby's breath prints for the eighties, palm tree prints for the sixties.

I ran my fingers over the smooth and bare walls and asked what color they wanted to be. I splashed some maroon on a wall, added the color of trees on another. An orange somewhere too. I took the color of the sea and threw it on as well. I didn't care about getting it on the floor; I was going to cover it soon anyway. The sea gray joined the splatters of orange and maroon on the wooden floorboards, the shag carpet long gone. The laminate I would use as flooring sat on the porch, and it bowed under its weight.

I stared at the mosaic of color, eyeing each shade, listening for Jerry's whisper, a "this one" or "pick that one." But there was nothing. None of the colors spoke to me. I sank into my chair and watched the dust fall from the chandelier, hoping it would swirl around one of the colors and make the decision for me.

I liked the maroon. I liked the orange. But neither seemed right. It was like one was trying to be the other, so I helped them out. I didn't have a clean stick, so I used my hands, mixing the red into the orange and the orange into red, and a burnt orange sunset blossomed in my hands. I couldn't wait. I smeared the color on the wall. My heart swelled. It was a sunset I managed to bring inside.

I could hear Jerry laugh, and I thought I saw the chandelier flicker. A smile from him. I smiled too, and it felt like I could finally breathe. My hands shook, but I scooped up the sun and smeared it on the walls, coating the sea and trees I'd foolishly tried to bring in. I'd have to go over it again with a brush to smooth out the lines, but the idea of spreading the sun and making Jerry smile made me frantic. I wanted him to be happy.

"I am," he said.

"I just want you to love this house."

He didn't say anything, so I scooped up more of the

paint and moved to the next wall. I used my fingers to push the paint into the corners. I covered the trim. I could fix that later. In the end, the floor was as orange as the walls.

I sat back on my green velvet chair, sunset color drying on my arms. I loved it. The chandelier flickered again. I knew Jer Bear loved it too.

I wanted to get the cracking paint off my skin and opted to go for a walk on my stretch of the beach. I didn't wear shoes. I told myself it was on purpose. I walked through the sand and let the water run over my feet and told myself it was because it was what I wanted. I bent down and used the wet sand to scrub the paint from between my fingers and up my arms and to my elbows. I used the coarse sand to scrub my skin raw.

I walked back to the house but ended up at my bench instead. It still felt warm from the last time I was there. I felt the *thing* with me. Despite my numb feet, I knew they were cut up. I watched the waves from my new vantage point and let my hands hang. The tips of my fingers brushed the tops of the wildflowers.

I breathed in the sweet scent of the flowers and salt. The wind rustled the petals and tickled my fingertips. I loved those. I *really* loved those. I picked a few stalks from the bushes and breathed them in. Lavender. Why didn't I realize this was lavender earlier?

These were my favorite, but they just didn't smell like I remembered. I willed the lavender-scented oxygen to push their memories into my blood. I willed the blood to carry the memories of flowers and happier times to my brain.

My stomach sank when I walked back into the house to find the sunset paint fading into a much more muted and mellow color. I pried open the can of paint and set to mixing the colors. When that burnt orange bloomed, I coated the walls again. I couldn't help but stare at my hands as they moved up and down the walls. I thought they had more wrinkles, maybe deeper too. The orange settled into the small canyons. No rivers yet, no scars, but I was only just beginning this house. I shoved globs of the orange paint into the large cracks, gluing the house back together with paint and color.

I sat back in my chair, inhaling the paint fumes, and watched the walls dry, taking care not to blink. The wet turned to matte and turned into the wall itself. I eyed the shadow within the walls, chasing it from kitchen to living room.

I grew tired of dancing over the spots of orange paint on the ground, so I swept the floors again and flung open the double doors, setting up my little workstation just beyond the threshold on the porch. A slab of wood across two sawhorses made the perfect table, and I set to work unwrapping the packages of flooring.

After lining a few rows up, I marked where I wanted the cut and plugged in the little hand saw. It chewed up the first few pieces, and I chucked them into the dumpster. I clenched my jaw. Embarrassment rose within me, and my blood bubbled. I was alone; I shouldn't care, but I did. After a few more tries, I got it right. I snapped each piece in place, a few fingernails too, but it was worth it.

The clean boards looked like they were made for this seaside cottage.

I had to use a hammer on the edges and ended up splintering a board, and I had to cut the piece all over. I looked at the finished two rows and let a tear spill to the orange, paint-splattered floor. It was crooked, the lines uneven. I shouldn't have been surprised with how uneven the house was. It would look better when the whole floor was done.

That ugly chandelier mocked me. I screamed profanities just to walk out the front door and cut another piece. And another. And another. And my hand. I was halfway through snapping in another piece when I spotted the constellation of red droplets on the floor mixing with the orange paint.

I ran to the kitchen despite my aching knees and wrapped my hand in a towel. I grabbed another and worked to scrub the red from the beautiful orange. I scrubbed the red *into* the orange, making some sick sunset on my floor. I didn't think my hand hurt. I didn't clean it. Instead, I let my blood seep into the pores of the house and prayed it would breathe it to life.

THE GHOST

She sat in her chair like she did every morning. I was surprised she managed to find a coffee cup. She stared at the chandelier and orange walls and half-finished floor.

The cut on her hand was mostly healed, and I was sure she was eager to get back to the flooring. If anything, just to check something off her list.

"Get out," she said.

"No," I said.

"You're not Jerry." She stared up at the gaudy and dusty chandelier.

"No."

"Leave my house." She didn't seem afraid.

"How did you know I was here?" I asked.

"The dust never settles. This house breathes."

"Fair enough." I sighed, letting my shadow cast long against the wall. She didn't scream. I didn't expect her to, but I was still disappointed.

"You're not real." She rubbed her eyes. "I'm just so tired."

And that was our first conversation. She picked at the skin around her nails, frequently glancing up at the dancing dust, to the chandelier, and back at her nails. When she was tired of peeling her own skin, she went back to the walls and continued peeling away the layers of the house.

"807 Friends Way, Rockaway City," she mumbled, over and over.

We walked across the beach, like we did every morning. I walked next to her instead of behind now. She could feel me by her side. I could see her glance at where my feet would have been. We searched for whole shells; the low tide finally exposed the little treasures, layers of waves peeling back, and unveiling fresh finds.

She eyed a whole sand dollar. She picked up the circle and stared at it. There was only a small crack down the middle. Then she looked to her bandaged hand and threw the shell back into the ocean.

"What are you really looking for?" I asked.

She shrugged and picked up an average rock. She pretended to examine it and chucked it in the water after she was done. We walked to our bench. She pulled the sweater around her, and we watched the tide come back in. She fiddled with the broken shells in her pocket. Her kids called her monthly, each one doing their duty of "checking in." Five calls just weren't enough for her, but she didn't know that.

"Do you know what day it is?"

"No." She looked for her phone, but she didn't have it and chose not to remember she forgot where it was.

"Does that bother you?"

"Not anymore."

Her summer tan was already faded, and the leaves turned yellow. Her hair was probably longer now, but I hadn't seen it down in weeks. Maybe months? Did I know what day it was?

She fumbled with the shells, trying to remember why she picked up the broken pieces. She threw one in the water.

"Tell me about Jerry," I tempted her.

"He lived a good life. A full one. He was happy."

"And?"

"He was everything, my high school sweetheart." She

threw a shell into the ocean. "Married when we were barely twenty." She threw another. "I was a teacher while we tried for babies. Lord, that took, what? A decade. But they came in their own time." She threw another shell into the waves. "Then he worked, I mothered, and we never left that little town. And when the kids left, it didn't feel the same, so we got this place." She threw another broken shard. "But he left me, and I'm all alone, and I don't know who I am." She threw the fistful of bleached shells back where they came from.

"I understand."

She pursed her lips. "What's your name?"

"I have no name," I lied.

"You do," she said.

"I go by many these days," I confessed. "Maybe I am like you too, forgetting who I am."

"You're a thief."

"What does Jerry look like?" I asked.

"He has a gray beard," she whispered.

Had. "What did his laugh sound like? What did he smell like?"

"You stole that from me."

If I had a mouth, I would have smiled.

We walked through the crunching leaves and dead pine needles. She walked through her front door and was greeted by a crooked floor and sunset walls. She searched her wingback chair. After the floor had been finished, she took great care to place it exactly where she had originally found it, not wanting to change her view of the chandelier.

She searched the kitchen, then her bedroom, with her worn mattress she had finally pulled from the storage container. It sat on the dusty floor, getting ruined. She didn't find what she was looking for in the nest of blankets and twisted sheets, so she searched the chair again.

"You lost it," I reminded her.

"I need it."

"Why?"

"I'm not so sure he has a beard; I need a picture."

We searched for the rest of the evening. And when she sat in her chair and stared at the chandelier, I approached with my deal. "I can help you remember," I lied.

"How?"

"An exchange, goods and services for a crisp dollar."

"Jerry used to say that."

"See? Already remembering."

"Did he have a beard?" she asked.

"Maybe. You need to find out."

"Where is my phone?"

"Why do you need it? To look up pictures and pretend to remember? What happens when you forget who the man in the picture is?"

She stared at the chandelier. Dust floated down and settled on the floor. There was still blood in the cracks of the new laminate.

"The dust can look like snowflakes, see?" I said, and her eyes followed a spec down from the ceiling. It landed in her lap. "Winter is coming."

She was out of her chair in a flash, and I was on her heels, chasing her down the path, beyond the beach and to our bench. She sat as still as before. Her hand fell to her side, letting the wildflowers and lavender brush up against her fingers. "These aren't my favorite. I love tulips."

"I think you're right," I said.

"I smell tulips in the air," she said as we walked back to the house.

I think I smelled them too.

She had just sat in her wingback chair when the phone in her pocket rang.

"Hello," she answered.

"Hey Mom," Auggie said.

"Oh hi! How are things going for you, eating all that chocolate?"

"I'm not in Germany anymore, remember? Moved bases and I'm in Japan, but June is there, remember? In France? Teaching."

"Right, right, I got the chocolates from June, but for some reason, I think they come from you still," she lied. She looked to the top of the fridge where she hid the half empty box of chocolate truffles.

"It's okay, I just wanted to call and check-in. Couldn't sleep so I figured it was meant to be, time changes and all."

The woman walked to the refrigerator and reached her hand up, blindly searching for the box. "Well, that's mighty thoughtful. I miss you."

"I miss you too, how's the house? Haven't gotten many updates lately."

I could see her searching her mind, what was left of it, and coming up with some excuse. Something, anything to say. Her face was pure panic. "Oh, it's coming along, much slower than I thought it would, but I'm enjoying the process."

"Have new friends in that little town of yours?"

"A few," she lied again and glanced at the chandelier, pulling her hand from the top of the fridge. She looked around the counters, scanning for the box of chocolates. She wouldn't find any.

"I'm sorry we can't make it this year." He sighed a long, drawn out breath, like he had been holding it the whole conversation. "I know June is pretty bummed too."

"No, no, no," the woman said, frantically scribbling a note on the wall. "I understand. The house really isn't fit for guests anyways. The kids would be bored too."

"It's just, we said we could make it last year and couldn't. This will be the second Christmas alone in that house for you."

Second? Had it really been that long?

The woman bit her lip. It looked like it was news to her too.

"I have some old friends I spend my time with now, relax. You worry too much. This house—this project, it has been good for me." She scowled at the walls, trying to find me.

Auggie laughed. "Call June, I know she's feeling bad, but they're working her hard at the university over there."

"Will do," the woman said, scribbling another note in pencil across the wall.

He said some other things, but she missed it, trying to get all her notes down before he hung up. When he did, she stared at her ledger.

No Christmas last year, call June. Chocolates? No Christmas this year.

She pulled out her phone, stared at the screen, and set it back down. She looked at the other notes, scribbled on the walls in pencil. "Chocolates? Who stole my chocolate?"

She continued searching for the missing package. She had a television and a stand for it now, which she searched top to bottom. Nothing. She searched her bedroom, mattress on the floor, only to give up when she forgot what she was looking for.

I followed her throughout the house, enjoying her nerves, and enjoying it even more when she forgot why she was nervous.

"I know you're the one stealing my chocolates," she said.

"How can you know that?" I asked.

"Who else is here?"

"Just us, I suppose," I whispered.

She stared at the scar on her hand. "You know, I don't really remember what they look like?" She almost laughed. I could tell when a laugh got stuck in her throat.

"What would you like to remember?"

"That is like asking a child where they lost their favorite toy."

"And yet, they always have an answer."

"I want to remember what he looks like," she said.

"Done."

"I still don't remember. Did he have a beard?" She picked at the scabs on her hands, making little red rivers over them. The blood trickled down her fingers, then she wiped them on her pants. She created sunsets wherever she went.

"You will see," I lied. "Just go about your day. It will all come to you."

Her eyes darted from shadow to shadow. She saw me in some; she saw Jerry in some. She trudged the steps upstairs, not bothering to give a glance at the chandelier. She washed the grime from her cuts and shed her clothes on the bathroom floor. She filled the tub with water and dipped her tired bones in. She sat in the warmth until it sapped the cold from her. She heard the voices downstairs, and she had finally decided to muster the strength to stand.

Her eyes lit up; she stole a glance of herself in the mirror from the tub. She wetted her hair with the soapy water and frowned. She ran her fingers through the thin strands and frowned again.

"Just a minute," she yelled, and her excitement grew. I could see it in her quick breathing. She wrapped the towel around herself and frantically searched the sparse drawers, slicing her palm open on a sharp nail in the closet. She dabbed on some amber liquid and ran her fingers through her hair again, fresh streaks of blood coated some of the white strands. She cursed and wiped a towel over the open cuts. They refused to close.

"I'll be right down," she called again.

The voice grew louder, deep and rumbling. Others joined in. He used to have guests over quite often and unexpectedly. I suppose she assumed it was the same situation. She trotted to her room and searched the small closet. She wrote a note on the wall with the pencil she kept on the only little table in the room.

Fix closet door hinge.

She scribbled it under the other running list of to-dos and to remember. She searched the few clothes hanging and opted for the only dress hanging, black, with worn spots on the knees. She checked her list. No notes about the dress, so she stepped into it and did her best to zip it herself. She sat on the end of the bed, listening to the voices below her.

I waited for her to descend the steps, but she didn't. Instead, she stayed still, like a statue and listened. She fell back, and her eyes fluttered closed, falling asleep to voices echoing below her.

The memories flooded her brain through the night, and I didn't feel bad about giving her ones she never asked for.

THE WOMAN

I was lying on the old mattress and a mass of blankets on the floor. I stretched my arms out, looking for the body that should have been next to me. Even after these months, I expected him to be here. Or was it years? The edges of the bed were cold and, once again, I was thrust into a sea of isolation. He should have been there. But he wasn't. They should be here, but they can't.

My right hand still had a towel over it, stuck to the top with dried blood. *Glue.* I peeled away the dirty towel and stared at the lines. Splinters jutted out. I rubbed my head, a constant hangover without the pleasure of the journey. I rubbed my eyes and stood. I found myself in my funeral dress. It was supposed to be rags by now. I tore it off and threw it against the wall. I stood in the cold room with just my socks on, and I felt a new shame wash over me.

But I didn't know why.

I dressed in my jeans and sweater and made my way to the bathroom, where I went through my own little routine of brushing my teeth and washing my face. I tried not to worry about the state of my mangy hair.

"You never had to worry about it," it told me.

"Shut up." It did. After a moment I said, "You lie."

"Did I? Or did you forget again?" it asked.

I hated that shadow.

"Then why do you talk to me?"

It mocked me. "Shut up," I said. It listened to me.

"No, I didn't," it said.

"SHUT UP!"

The phone rang. I searched for it, eventually finding it under the clawfoot bathtub, still full of soap and grime. I reached my hand in the cold water and watched it drain. Flecks of dried blood being sucked away.

"Hello?"

"Hey, Mom."

"Hey!" I said. "June?" I just to make sure.

"Yeah," she laughed, and it made my heart jump into my throat.

"I miss you," I blurted out. I tried not to sound too needy, but it was hard.

"Miss you too. Look, it's pretty late over here, but I just found out and wanted to let you know. I can call back, and we can go talk about it more later."

"Okay," I started, but I raced to the bedroom where I grappled for the pencil intent on running away from my fingers.

"Well, I was just offered a full-time faculty position at the university over here. No more adjunct life!"

"That's amazing, June Bug! Congratulations, your father is going to be so proud."

"Yeah, he would be." She cleared her throat.

My hand was poised, holding the pencil. I really needed to get a paper pad. The walls would fill up.

"Mom, did you hear me?"

"What?"

"I said I need to start prepping for the spring quarter."

"I see." I still wasn't sure what to write.

"What?" she asked.

"I said, I still don't know what to write."

"Mom, is the connection bad or something? I'll call back tomorrow, but I just wanted to let you know sooner than later that I won't be able to make it for Christmas."

The phone hung up. I'm not sure if I did it or she did.

I paced, whispering, "Christmas, Christmas, Christmas," and eventually I found it in the kitchen. The note on the wall. I cross it out. Three "Christmas" notes crossed out now.

"They haven't seen the house yet," it reminded me.

"I know," I said. "Probably a good thing. Look at this mess."

The shadows moved, and I knew it agreed with me. I spent my time reapplying the orange paint to the walls. It just faded so fast.

The coffee maker beeped, and I thanked the ghost for being thoughtful enough to put some on.

"I didn't," it teased.

I sipped the coffee. It wasn't as warm as I usually liked it.

I caught a glimpse of it, *the thing*, slithering across the floor. I grabbed the broom and smacked it down on it before it could float away. I pinched it between my fingers.

"I told you to quit this madness!" I bellowed. I let the soft strand of silver slip from my fingers, hoping it would land in the shadows and *the thing* would be forced to look at it. "Well?" I repeated.

"Wasn't me."

"Quit lying," I said. "You cut my hair." I checked my hair—it was still there—but I knew *it* cut it at night.

"I never lie," it said.

I searched my notes on the wall and couldn't find anything to tell me if it is true or not.

"You're whispering again," it said.

I didn't answer. I continued scanning the corners for more of what it stole from me. I got distracted by the note on the wall. I'd meant to check this earlier. Auggie. I closed my eyes and tried to place a name with the face. The ghost pushed the button on my phone for me and it rang.

"Hello?" Auggie answered.

"Hi! Yes," I said. "Just wanted to call and see how it's going over there for you." I thought *over there* was vague enough.

"Things are going," he said. "Marla is doing fine. We went and watched the kiddos in their school play the other day. You haven't called in a while."

He paused and waited for me to say something equally interesting, and I froze. I searched the scribbles on the walls for clues. When I wait too long, he asked, "What have you been doing over there? What did you do last night?"

I grasped the olive branch and clung to it. Last night, only hours ago. "Well, I had some people over," I said.

"You lie," it whispered in my other ear.

"Hush," I mouthed.

"Oh, how fun. Got a good little group of friends over there now. It's been what? Three years?" Auggie asked.

"Almost," I said, but I scribbled the number down for me to double-check later. "And yeah, had some friends over last night. We just visited." I was sure that's what happened. The ghost didn't say anything. Maybe I was right.

"Are they still over now?" Auggie asked. "I think I hear people."

"No, I think I have a bad connection. June Bug called earlier and said something like that."

"Oh, okay," he said.

We chatted a little more about this and that. I told him about my friends, mostly about the one I saw most often. I explained how he was rather shy, but as still in good shape, nimble and quick, and always there with a witty remark. I told him how we went on walks to my bench and how we watched the sea. I told him he lived close, even though I didn't know if that was true or not. I saw the ghost smile as I explained this, but I ignored it.

"Look Mom, I gotta run. Time zones are strange, and we are just sitting down for dinner."

"All right then." I thought he could hear my smile. *Mom.* That was my boy.

I checked the wall one last time for anything I might have missed. I didn't see anything. I went back to painting that lovely shade of orange across the walls.

"You already painted that spot," the ghost said.

"I missed a spot."

"Soon the walls will have so many layers they will close in around you and keep you trapped here," it chuckled.

"They already do."

I picked up my feet and ran. I sprinted to the beach and kicked off my shoes in the sand, and like a child bounding to the waves, I raced to a rolling and roaring sea. I crashed into it and let the cold, salty sting wash over me. I held my breath and forced myself under. I opened my mouth and let the water fill my throat. I screamed and pushed it out again. Salt stung my eyes. I thought about inhaling, forcing the water into my lungs. It could have been that simple. A sharp breath of the cold sea and it would be over, no burials needed. No damned orange tulips. I'd float away, leaving an unfinished house and chocolates somewhere.

And I saw June Bug walking down her own coastline. I'd float across the ocean, the currents, and wash up on her own shore. Maybe I'd wash up on Auggie's doorstep. I'd be long gone. My skin would be eroded and melted away, food for the fish. But she'd recognize me. I wouldn't want her to see that. So, I forced myself up.

I fought the ocean's embrace and managed to stand, only to be knocked over by another wave. It pulled at my heels and sucked me under. The pressure around me crushed the air from me. I clawed my way to the surface. The sandy shore was yards away. My jeans were soaked, acting as weights, rooting me down. The ghost watched me struggle.

"You wanted this," it shouted over the waves.

"Not like this," I cried. *On my own terms.*

The current's tentacles wrapped around me and pulled me under again. The thunder of the waves beating the sand echoed in my ears.

And then all was still.

For a moment, I was content, suspended in the vibrations of the waters, but it jarred something loose, and I climbed my way out. I reached for the ghost's hand, but it didn't move.

I forced my shaking legs to carry me beyond the reach of the rolling waves, and I collapsed in the sand. I only had to open my lips the barest bit for the air to rush in and inflate my crushed lungs. It burned like whiskey. The sand smelled like whiskey too.

And the water lapped over me, spilling onto the floor. I was in the bathtub, whiskey in hand, lips just above the surface. The salt I tasted came from the ocean behind my eyes.

"807 Friends way," I whispered.

The rain hit the window, and the drops ran down the glass, creating rivers and veins on this living house.

THE GHOST

Dear June Bug and Auggie Boy,

I hope this letter finds you well. I'm sure it will, at some point, eventually. Probably. Everything is a probably. There are a thousand roads in the ocean, but you two move around enough that I am sure it will find you. Or maybe it won't.

I just wanted to let you two know that your mother has died. I was once part of this world, but I can see that it is not the world fading, but myself. And I don't think anyone else knows that I am fading from this place.

I am dead but somehow living. It is hard to know your mind is dying and memories leaking out when your body is still breathing.

But take comfort in knowing that, if I wait a minute, I will forget this pain.

I just wanted to let you know that I love you both. I wanted to say that before your faces escaped my own mind.

. . .

She folded the note. She took her time on it, making sure each line was even and neat. She wrote and rewrote it several times over. The bare spaces of the walls were filled with this letter to no one.

I scanned the walls, I knew she saw me. She wasn't afraid. They never were at the end. I sat in the wing back chair, which was more comfortable than it looked, and settled in, still watching her draft the notes on the wall. She held her breath as she wrote, holding the paper against the wall, nearly tracing over her perfect writing. When we were satisfied, she folded it neatly and buried it in her pocket. I smiled and nodded, and I think she found some sense of relief, at least, her shoulders slumped and her hands shook less.

I moved and allowed her to take her seat in the chair. We watched the chandelier's shadow on the floor.

"Do you think he will come tonight?" she asked.

"Only one way to find out," I said.

I really didn't have it in me to tell her it was still morning. But she went upstairs anyway and readied herself for the bed. I left the TV on again, and she fell asleep to the sound of voices below her. She smiled when the voices from the sitcom wafted to her ears, and for a moment, I was happy for her. It was like watching a child finally wrestle themselves to sleep on their own, a new stage in their development.

She slept in that cloud of grief. She breathed in darkness, and it ate away at her. The woman's insides turned black and died, the disease coursing through her and settling in her brain. Her phone rang from the cushions downstairs. She didn't hear it.

The television's voice convinced her she was not alone, and she finally pulled herself into a deep sleep. I slid into the walls and ate some chocolate.

10

MAGPIES

"Come quick," Granny screeched from the window. "Get your ass over here."

I steeled myself and joined her at her elbow.

"You're too late, brainless girl." Spittle flew from her loose and sagging lips. "He's flown away. Gone now."

"What?" I wiped the wet from my face. "A bird?"

"Yes. A magpie. And *only* I saw him. Now sorrow will come our way." She rounded on me. "And it's all *your* fault. Stupid, no good thing, you are." She reeked of vodka, that clear liquid Granny always claimed was water. It was poison. She always found more of the stuff, even after Mom threw out her bottles, and it always made her fangs show worse.

Mom said I had to be nice, even *kind*. But it was like trying to play with a snake. She was too fast and wicked for me. It was not a fair fight. A snake wouldn't be *kind* to me.

"I bet someone dies." She licked the venom from her

lips. "Someone's going to die, and you'll be the one to blame because you were too busy sitting on your fat cheeks to get over here and see it in time."

I didn't believe any of her nonsense, the hag. It was funny though; Granny had a heart attack that night. She was lying in one of those cold and itchy beds in the hospital now. Mom said things didn't look too good for her. The snake had finally gone belly up. It was just a coincidence, but it did make me wonder.

I always did like magpies.

11

PEELING POTATOES

T he girl bounded up the steps as fast as her twelve-year-old legs would carry her. The sun was beginning to dip and create long shadows across the dried grass. She sprinted away from the shadow's hands, hoping she was fast enough so the fingers wouldn't pull her into the darkness. She clutched the plastic bucket with both hands. "Think I have enough?"

Meemaw thumbed through the cherries and tossed a few out. "Lots of these have the devil in 'em."

"What?"

"See here, Darby, there are holes in nearly all of 'em. The little devils get in there and rot it from the inside to the out."

"So, we can't use them?"

Meemaw pulled a few of the bright red cherries onto her lap. "Some are good, just look carefully now and help me sort. Don't want making no tart with little devils in them."

Darby nodded and used the last bit of light from the sun to inspect for the little devils.

"What would happen if you ate one?" Darby asked.

Meemaw cackled and stood, cradling the cherries in her apron. "If I ate one? It would probably shrivel up and die. I am mostly piss and vinegar, you know. That's not too good for devils."

Darby wrinkled her nose. Neither piss nor vinegar seemed a good thing to eat. *But if it killed a devil...*

"But you," Meemaw pinched Darby's cheek, "You're made of sugar and honey. The little devils would eat you right up, make *you* rot from the inside out."

Darby's stomach turned. "What if someone was half and half?"

Meemaw shrugged and waited for Darby to open the screen door. "I don't know."

They went in and made a cherry tart. A devil-free tart.

"Now stay put with your Meemaw until I get back," Darby's father shouted as he walked out the door. He called over his shoulder, "Ma, she's in big trouble. Got a call from the school again. Make her peel potatoes until she never wants to think about using her hands for violence again."

"Oh dear." Meemaw rounded on Darby, staring at her with an expression that could have made a demon wilt.

Those devils were dead long before she ate them. Darby shoved her hands in her pockets.

"What did you do now?"

"Nothing!"

"That ain't what your teacher said." Meemaw rolled up her sleeves and put her hands on her hips. "Now what did your hands do?"

"Nothing," Darby said. "It was that girl Sandy. She was throwin' rocks from the schoolyard at passing cars. I was just close enough to get in trouble too."

Meemaw gave the girl a little knife. "Here. Get to peelin' that bag."

Darby did, nearly cutting her thumb a few times in the process. They listened to the radio and peeled the skin away to the beat of Elvis's songs. Meemaw hated that new singer but always happened to have him playing when Darby was helping in the kitchen.

They got to an old bag of russet potatoes, and Meema broke the quiet with her muttering. "Oh dear, this bag is old. Look at all those eyes. These are so green they almost match your own eyes. Don't worry, yours are prettier." She held a particularly green-looking potato next to Darby's head. "Same shade of hazel."

Darby laughed, and she almost forgot she was supposed to be pouting. "What are those?" She pointed to the green bits and sprouts.

"The eyes? They grow when a tater is old. Gotta be real careful and cut them off real nice and clean. The green parts can make people sick. I even heard the old lady down the road ate too many and had to go to the hospital."

"Really?"

Meemaw smiled. "No, but it makes for a good story right? But seriously, they can make people sick, especially the old and young, which we both are. So it be best to cut the green away real perfect."

Darby followed Meemaw's lead and was generous with her cuts, removing the green stalks poking out of the potatoes and leaving no trace of the eyes.

"Meemaw? Do the devils really make someone rot from the inside?"

Meemaw laughed. "Devils?"

"In the cherries."

Meemaw cackled again. "Those were just worms. You know that."

Darby chuckled. "Yeah, I just thought it was funny."

And when Meemaw wasn't looking, Darby pocketed a few of the eyes, the especially green ones.

When her father came home, she was sent to bed with no supper on account of her rock throwin' shenanigans. Once in her room, she wrapped the green bits in a cloth and placed it in her school bag because she was tired of them staring at her. She hoped the eyes would fester and grow more potent overnight.

When the morning came, she snuck a peek at them, and they winked at her. *These would do just fine. Much better than the little devils did.*

At school, when the lunch bell rang and the chaos of kids surrounded her, Darby made her way to the cafeteria. She slid open her lunch ; it was a brown paper bag. Sandy sat across from her with a shiny tin lunch pail.

"Darby, Darby. Whatcha got today? More of those cherry tarts? Maybe a cookie?" Sandy said.

"Just a sandwich," Darby mumbled. She slid her lunch across the table before she made a scene like last time. Sandy took a big bite of the jam sandwich, just like she had done every day, a little eye poking out from the crust. The worms didn't work, but maybe an evil eye would do the trick.

12

SPLITTING HEADACHE

He sat on his mother's porch, smoking a cigarette. The first puff of the morning felt a lot like the first time he'd had one. A sweet relief. He had been what —thirteen the first time? It was behind the school during lunch, and though he had been suspended, no one questioned his guts after that. It was a currency more valuable than gold. But you could never be too rich, so he chugged a bottle of vodka the week he got back, also behind the school. Vodka never tasted the same.

Zeke puffed on the cigarette a second time, and he was brought back into his thirty-year-old body. He watched as the neighbor paced the street wearing his usual jeans, but slippers? That was new. He normally had a dog with him, a scrappy-looking mutt. The neighbor scratched his skin, blood drying under his nails. "I can't get it out," he mumbled over and over.

The man walked to where Zeke sat. "Help me," the

neighbor whispered, pounding on his scalp with his fist. "I can't get it out."

"What, you got lice or something? Maybe gnats?"

"It's not, I can't get it out." The man had scratched his scalp bloody, the flesh torn away on one side. He made a decent dent in his scalp too.

"Sure. I can help you out." Zeke stood and stepped on the cigarette. "Follow me."

He wasn't sure why, but the man looked to be in so much pain. The blood was beginning to dribble down his neck and stain his white shirt. Zeke was never one to get squeamish; he had the guts after all. So he led the man, still scratching at his scalp, to the woodpile around back.

"Here," Zeke said, taking the ax from its spot on the chopping block. "This might help."

"Thank you." The man stopped his incessant scratching and moved to chewing his lip. He took the ax from Zeke and gripped the handle with his bloody fingers and held it tight. Then he dropped it. "I can't do it." He started scratching again. "I am so close to getting it out, can you do it?"

"Can I?"

"Yeah." The man pointed at the ax.

"Sure," Zeke said, picking the ax up, ignoring the warm, bloody fingerprints. It was sticky. He looked up to find the man stretching his head out, leaving a wide berth for Zeke to swing the ax and split his skull, no doubt the man's end goal here.

Zeke held it, ready to let it fall through the air. Really,

it would be gravity's doing, Zeke was just aiming. And then he couldn't.

"I'm sorry," Zeke said to the man. "I just can't." He'd never had his guts go soft before.

The man only nodded and shuffled away, muttering, "I gotta get it out."

"Gotta get it out..." Zeke whispered and shuffled back into his mom's house, mumbling something about breakfast, scratching his head.

And it never stopped itching. His scalp tickled and burned, begging his nails to break the skin.

"I have an idea," he explained to his mom at the dinner table that night. It had been nagging him all day.

"Now I'm scared." His mom laughed and shoved some chili in her mouth.

"No," Zeke said, scratching at his scalp through his thick, brown hair. "It's just not coming to me."

"Well, give it a minute."

"No." He scratched harder, trying to jar the thought loose, maybe help dig it out. "It's like when you forget a word, ya know? Like right on the tip of your tongue? But it's not coming to me. I just need to get it out."

And all through dinner, the idea of something poked at him, and he was determined to find the *something*. He went to bed thinking it could stave off the feeling of forgetting the something by sleeping. He fell asleep muttering, "I just gotta get it out..." Except he never fell asleep.

The idea continued to pound at his skull from the inside, trying to break out from the bone. Zeke scratched his scalp and felt a moment's elation when the blood got sticky on his hands. He was close to freeing the thing.

But the idea? The memory, the *thing*, just pounded away from inside. Beating his skill like a drum, over and over and over. And when the sun broke the black night, he went out for his morning cigarette, pulling on some jeans and ignoring the sweatshirt he usually went for. The cold didn't faze him at all.

He sat in this regular spot, forgetting to light the cigarette and puffed on air, scratching and itching and pulling at the skin on his scalp. When the pounding grew to be too much, he paced the front, marching to the rhythm of the drumming in his head. "I just need it out."

The idea was *there*, so close, the migraine threatening to split him in two, and he knew he would get no relief until this thing was out.

"Hey," a voice called.

It made him jump, and the pounding grew worse, angry to have broken up the rhythm of itching and peeling away the skin. He was at the bone now. He scratched harder. "What?"

It was a student, so obviously a student, with his oversized backpack, giant coat, and lanyard. "Want any help with that—" The small student pointed to Zeke's side, at the sharp and shiny ax.

13

CLOSET

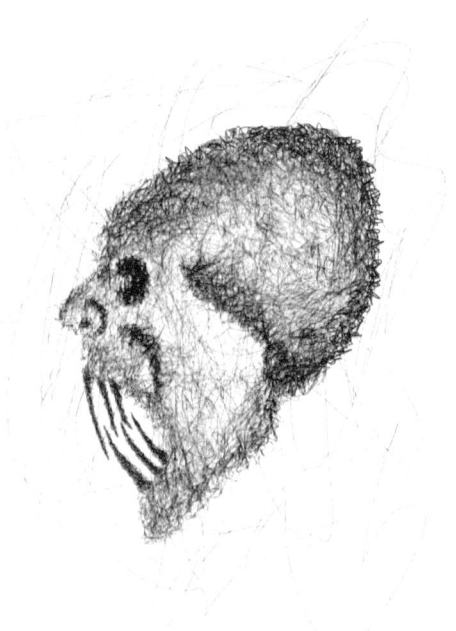

I was stuck inside a closet with a monster. "It's just five minutes," I whispered. The little closet was dark, and I felt the walls close in on me. I was careful not to touch anything in case it was the monster. He was probably slimy or sharp.

"How'd they trick you?" the monster asked.

The gaggle of girls laughed, and their shrill voices made their way into the tiny room. They didn't hear the voice of the *thing*. It was like quiet thunder, shaking my bones. I took a breath; the air was sour and dry. The monster and I exchanged oxygen between our lungs.

If it breathed at all. Maybe it didn't have lungs.

"Nothing to say?" it asked again. "Too scared? But not too scared to spend five minutes with me."

"They didn't trick me," I said. Screw my earlier rules. I let my back lean against a wall. The rough wood from the old house poked my spine as I slid to the ground. Better than trying to stand. It was too dark; it made me dizzy. Like I was underwater, and I didn't know which way was up.

"Yet you are in here. And they are out there."

"I know," I said.

"How'd they get you in here?"

I thought I heard it lick its lips like it was going to devour me. At least I'd be a story the girls could use. I'd live on in their words, through their "I was there" stories. I almost wished he'd bite me.

"What? You didn't want to dance around and look like a fool for their attention, so you agree to this?"

"I don't dance," I admitted.

"What do you want?"

"I don't know," I whispered, casting a glance to the little door that had been barred shut. I still heard the girls out there, talking, chatting, all without me. They'd get the butterflies in their stomachs when the time drew near. The clock ticked loud throughout the little basement. I could hear it through the walls and the monster's heavy breathing. Probably four minutes left.

"What do you want?" it asked again.

"I don't know." I shrugged even though I knew it couldn't see me. Or maybe it could.

"I think you are willing to trade parts of yourself for their acceptance."

"Bold," I said. *True*, I thought.

The air in the little closet warmed. It was sticky, like I could reach out and mold a shape from the oxygen with my hands.

"I propose a trade," the monster whispered.

Three minutes now. Only three minutes. "Okay, what do you propose?" And I searched the folds of my brain for what would be worth making a deal with an unseen monster.

The girls laughed again, deep belly laughs. I ached. I wanted to laugh.

"You want to be one of them. To be accepted for who you are. No more ridiculous trials to keep their interest."

It didn't take a monster to see that.

"A trade," it said. "Your dignity and pride for their love and acceptance."

"Deal."

"It's done."

And my thumb hurt. It felt sticky and wet. Two minutes now. I didn't feel any different, save for an ember of hope in my chest and slick thumb.

One minute. The girls tapped on the door, waiting for me to emerge. They were giddy and excited over the prospect of something scary.

I got to my feet and fumbled for the handle. The darkness made it hard to breathe, like it was taking the last seconds to suffocate me. But the silent monster was more terrifying now. He had part of me. I supposed I had part of it.

"You know—" its voice cut through the air. "I make no pretense about what I am. I can claim honesty, but you? What do you have now? You're part monster, a fake. A false person walking. Tell me, what does that make you?"

"Human, I suppose." And I felt different.

The door swung open. The light nearly blinded me, and I left the monster in the dark, walking out to my friends. I glanced at my thumb; the blood was finally starting to dry. A blood promise.

"You'll be back," the monster said.

And I was afraid it was right.

14

THE SISTER

"Your mama home, girl?"

"No," The Girl said.

"Oh, I see." His fingers brushed over her hand as he dropped the mail into her palms.

She liked the way his hand felt. Better still, she liked the smile he gave her. Even better after that was the way his eyes glinted when she told him her mama was off somewhere.

"Maybe I'll see you around later." He smiled that winner smile, and she nodded.

It felt good to smile at him. It felt better when he smiled back.

She saw him later, just like he said she would. He was sitting on a bench at the park, licking an ice-cream cone. It made her shiver. The Girl held her little sister's hand, and she didn't smile at him because he smiled at *her*. He grinned at the little sister clutching The Girl's hand, the ribbons bouncing in her hair.

The Girl set her jaw and walked right on by. He never stopped his licking, even with the cream running down his hand. She tugged the little sister along, frustrated. She had been saving a smile just for him.

"You didn't smile at me yesterday," he said.

"I couldn't." She decided to meet him at the mailbox. The screaming from inside was embarrassing. Mama had too many of her drinks, and she was talking to the walls again. The little sister sat on the porch, drawing on the crumbling steps with a rock. She was too focused to notice, so The Girl gave him a smile. And he smiled back.

But he looked at the little sister on the porch.

The Girl frowned again and walked back to the house, mail in her hands.

"Think I could come in some time?" he asked.

She stopped her march back to the dilapidated single wide and thought for a minute. It would be nice. "No," she said, her back still to him. "Mama..."

"Maybe later."

She nodded and could feel his eyes on her neck.

"I'll see you later then," he called from his spot at the end of the yard, hand resting on the mailbox.

She turned and gave him a smile her little sister wouldn't see. "Yes."

"Mama says you'll go to hell," the little sister said. "Mama said Jesus will carve out your heart and feed it to the dogs."

"That won't happen." The Girl pulled her little sister by the hand into the woods. It was their usual retreat. Twenty-four cans gone usually meant twenty-four hours away from the house. Sometimes Mama would fall asleep, sometimes she wouldn't. And it wasn't worth taking a chance on the latter.

"Are we going to the creek?" the little sister asked.

"Yup," The Girl said, pulling the wide-eyed little thing along with her.

They squatted at their favorite spot, letting the sun smooth their goosebumps away. The Girl was thankful it was still summer. The night would be full of stars, and the frost wouldn't be there to bite at their feet.

"Thought I heard you two ladies out here splashing." It was the man's voice. His hands were in his pockets, and he sauntered through the trees, wearing that straight smile of his.

The Girl didn't try to hide her own grin this time.

"Is everybody decent?" he asked.

We never are. "Yes," The Girl laughed, toweling her little sister's hair with her sweater and straightening the little sister's mismatched ribbons.

"Too bad," the man laughed. He looked from The Girl's eyes to the legs of her little sister.

"What were you playing?" he asked.

"A game," the little sister said.

"We were gonna play another," The Girl said.

"Chase?" the man asked. He wore jeans and a flan-

nel, not his normal mailman uniform, and it made The
Girl's eyes linger over his exposed forearms.

"That could be fun," the little sister said.

"It could," The Girl said.

"Chase us," the little sister said, squealing as she took
off running.

And he did. He played at first. The Girl knew he
was fast, but he let the little sister think she was
winning. The man let them weave between the trees,
and The Girl tried not to be annoyed that his smile was
for the girl with ribbons. She touched her ribbon-less
hair and grabbed the little sister's hand. "We have to
go."

"It's time already?" the little sister asked.

The man pretended to be out of breath. "Already? I
just caught up."

"We have to go," The Girl said.

"I'll see you later then," the man said to her back.

She nodded and pulled her little sister along. It felt
like a real chase this time.

They were lucky. Mama was fast asleep on the sofa
when they crept back into the stuffy house. They snug-
gled tight in their bed, playing a quiet game of slapping
the fleas off each other's skin.

"Leave the window open," her little sister said.
"Maybe he'll come back to play."

The Girl made a mistake and left it open.

They lied on their backs and stared at the water-stained ceiling. Their own private set of constellations. "Do you really think Jesus will carve out our hearts?"

The Girl scoffed. "No, and even if he did, it doesn't hurt."

"How do you know?"

"I just do." The Girl pinched her little sister's side, and the little sister giggled.

"I thought I heard you two ladies," said the man from the window.

The little sister sat up, eyes bright with the anticipation of another game.

"What?" the man asked, climbing through the window. "No smile for me?"

The little sister beamed, already pulling out a mismatched deck of cards. The Girl figured she would want to play their strange version of "go fish." They had to amend and make up some rules when they figured out several cards were missing.

The man didn't even look at The Girl's face once he got inside. Instead, he softly stepped across the floor and sat with the little sister, picking at the cards, then picking at her dress, then picking at the skin on her legs.

"This looks funny," he pulled the sleeve of the little sister's dress down.

"What about this?" The Girl asked. She stood in front of the man and pulled both of her sleeves down, revealing much more of her chest than she had ever before.

The man stood and smiled. Finally he smiled at *her*. He stepped over the cards and the little sister. He tugged a little harder on the dress, pulling it down more.

The little sister still on the floor, cards covering her legs, looked wide-eyed at The Girl and the man. "What are—"

And her words were snapped off by the sound of a knife piercing skin. The Girl had to only reach behind her under her grimy pillow to find the handle. It took only a moment to sink it between his ribs. She swore she felt the vibration of a beating heart slow through the handle of the knife.

The man let out a moan, a wet, sloppy sound. He fell to his knees, then on that funny little deck of cards.

"I thought you said it doesn't hurt," the little sister said.

"It only hurts the bad ones."

"Will it hurt me?"

"No," The Girl said, staring at the dead man on the floor, blood soaking into the wood. "You're too good."

"Will it hurt you?" the little sister asked.

"I don't know."

15

FAMILY DINNER

"Tommy, seriously, I get sick every time I eat your mother's cooking. I literally cannot figure out why, but there is something that she uses that just does *not* agree with me."

"She just uses a lot of salt." He sat on the edge of their new bed, pulling on his socks. "A lot of people get bloaty when they aren't used to that much salt."

"It's not salt, and I don't think she likes me," Amy confessed.

"Stop that." He smiled that sweet smile she fell in love with. He stood and wrapped his arms around her, and she buried her face into his shoulder, breathing in his scent. She was still trying to figure out what it was. *Sandalwood?* "She just doesn't speak English, and well—we sprung it on her. She just needs time. I am the baby, after all."

That needled at her. "We've been married six

months now!" Amy pulled away and worked on applying her mascara.

Their life was like a game, constantly getting to know each other, catching up for lost time. She knew he was the youngest, but the way he said *baby* made her wrinkle her nose. He wasn't a baby.

"Okay, but your parents reacted the same way—*Hi mom and dad, it's Amy. I went on vacation and came back married. Hope that's okay!*—she just needs some time to get used to the idea is all." He laughed and pinched her butt.

"Okay fine." She rolled her eyes. "She gets a little grace."

"I'll meet you in the car. Don't forget tennis shoes. There's this awesome hike I want to show you once we get over there. We didn't get a chance last time."

She nodded, inwardly groaning at the idea of spending two hours in a car just to get sick off his mother's cooking then try to hike. She had managed to skip the hike last time; her stomach had been too riled up to even think of a small walk. Tommy didn't seem to be convinced until she vomited on the way home. Then he believed her.

They had gone out to the small town about once every other month since they came back from vacation and their whirlwind marriage. It was so cliché, that "love at first sight" thing. But it was true. He transferred companies and moved in with her. They redid the little condo, all new furniture and paint, and it felt like home when she laid her head down at night.

"Over there is where my uncle used to live. We used

to walk over and play in the creek in his backyard," he explained as they entered the sleepy little farming town.

She wanted to learn more about the place where he grew up, more about what he did in college and post-graduation, but that was a black spot. He rarely talked about it. Said he's lost his way in the corporate world, and meeting her on his spontaneous trip was the best change he needed. But his hometown? His childhood? That was an open book.

Their life now was like a little treasure hunt, stumbling upon new pieces of information about each other, new quirks and constant "I didn't know that!" exclamations. Life was never boring now.

"What made you want to leave?" Amy asked. She knew the answer; it was the reason he wouldn't move back.

"Only so many opportunities here. As beautiful as it is, which you will get to see later, there isn't a glass ceiling to break through. It's a thick brick ceiling that's pretty low. I would be stuck selling insurance like my uncle. I wanted more. And now I have you, and I sure as hell wouldn't drag you back to this place, despite the surrounding state parks and secret waterfalls."

"Secret waterfalls?" She grinned, and her eyebrows raised.

"Yep, I'll show you after dinner. It's a mile loop, and it takes you to a little creek. We veer off the path a bit and follow it to a cute little waterfall and natural pool. Gorgeous. It's my little secret." He laughed. "Okay, the family secret. My cousins found it when they were looking for a place to smoke."

She laughed and shook her head. His cousins were wild as adults. She could only imagine what they were like as rowdy teens.

She stared out the window, mentally calculating how she was going to make it through the evening. She couldn't handle the cramps and the cold sweats again. The occasional vomiting was the worst. *I know she is doing something to my food.* She had gotten sick the first time, but chalked it up to nerves, meeting in the in-laws for the first time and all that. The second time was strange. The third time? *Something* was going on. She wasn't going to be fooled a fourth time.

When they walked inside, her husband greeted his large family, all in Spanish, and other than the occasional "tia!" she understood nothing. *"Tia" means good, right?*

Tommy whispered in her ear, "She's all riled up, upset we were late." He winked, and they took a seat in front of their already heaping plates. Her mother-in-law tutted and tittered about, making sure everyone was seated just so. She was no more than five foot, but the way people reacted to the matriarch made her seem at least eight feet tall. The thread of Amy's poorly woven plan was slipping away as she tried to sit in another place, and her mother-in-law got all worked up and made her move seats.

She watched her husband smile and banter with some uncles—she guessed they were uncles—and she looked for an opening. Nothing. She decided she was making this up. The cold sweats and diarrhea were just symptoms of nerves. So, she cracked open a cold one and drank it, determined to relax and let her stomach enjoy the food. *Mind over matter. Right?*

Amy shoveled the tamales and rice into her mouth. The family's chatter died down as they all ate. She was thankful for the quiet. The Spanish language that swirled around her most of the evening made her drowsy, like her brain was working on overdrive to understand something she had no experience with. She was a fish out of water. A toddler watching the grownups talk.

"So, you going to take her on the same hike?" one of his aunts asked. Amy was more than thankful for the English.

"Yep," Tommy said, stuffing his face with tamale.

"Even after—"

"Yep," he cut her off. His face went a little pale— maybe he got a taste of the mystical "salt."

"After?" Amy mumbled, hoping he would elaborate, give her some sort of rope to hang on to. But he shook his head slightly and moved on to the next thing.

She focused on avoiding eye contact with her mother-in-law as she waited for the *salt* to do its magic. *But it won't. It's just nerves.* She was wrong.

Her stomach knotted and bubbled. Her face felt hot and flushed and then her body shivered with chills. She made it through dinner and even managed to get her shoes on for the hike, telling herself it was just nerves.

"The trailhead is a few blocks down, figured we could walk there."

Amy nodded, swallowing down the saliva and rising bile. She held Tommy's arm, and he chatted about how his cousin was thinking of leaving the family business and the drama it would bring. That's what they were talking about at dinner, apparently.

"And here is the trailhead. It's kind of overgrown and a bit slick. Watch your step. The waterfall should be full and flowing fast, thanks to this rain."

Amy nodded. She only made it a few steps before she vomited in the bushes. "I can't do this."

"What is going on?" he asked, turning back for her. "Is it a flu bug or something?"

"It's your mother's damn salt. Except it sure as hell isn't *salt*. She is doing something with my food."

The ride home was somber. She held a bowl in her lap and worked on getting her stomach settled. She stuck her nose out the open window and chewed on mint gum. None of those tricks helped.

"You didn't need to talk about my mom like that," Tommy mumbled, driving with one hand, avoiding her eyes. "I don't know what is going on, but that is a serious accusation. Her messing with your food."

"I just don't feel good." Amy rubbed her forehead. *He is sensitive with his mom. Got it. A Mama's boy.* "I'm sorry. I was upset." *Is this our first fight?*

He sighed. "I'm sorry. I just wanted to take you on that hike. I guess I just wanted you to get out and move. I thought it would make you feel better, and to get away from everyone."

She felt like an ass. "I'm sorry. I really do want to see it, and I think it would have been fun to escape everyone for a little. Next time." She patted his hand, trying to work the rising bile back down her throat.

And a month and a half later, they were on that familiar country road, heading back to the in-laws. It was someone's birthday this week. It was always someone's birthday. She had her hiking shoes on. They planned to get there early and hike before the barbeque. Tommy was still so excited to show her the secret spot. She secretly thought he'd been trying as some romantic gesture. He fidgeted with his pocket, and she was sure there was some little gift in it. Maybe that pair of earrings she'd been eyeing.

But they hit construction and were late. The family was already sitting down, and the usual greetings were made in haste as the sound of stomachs rumbling overtook the barking of dogs and obligatory greetings. They sat in their usual spots. But Amy wasn't going to have a repeat.

It was easier than she thought. It took only a moment. When Tommy was giving his mama a kiss on the cheek, she switched the plates. Tommy's meal was in front of her, and Tommy would get to sample the special salt.

And dinner was the best she'd ever had. Her stomach was still, quiet. She could enjoy the tacos and tamales. She could breathe easy, and she was actually ready for the hike when things finally quieted. The piñatas had been smashed, and she was more than ready to burn off the extra slice of cake .

But the cramps hit him, and they went home early. She felt only slightly guilty. She drove home, relieved not to be holding a puke bowl and looking green. His cold sweats and cramps kept him up all night, but she slept like a child.

It was in the morning when the guilt hit her, and she confessed.

"You did what?" He gritted his teeth, and spittle flew from his mouth.

This flash of anger made her recoil. She took an involuntary step back. "She, well, I just wanted you to—"

"*She* did this?"

He called her, and the next hour was screams and chattering in Spanish.

Tommy's mother cried loud through the speaker, "Sé que mataste a esa otra esposa. No dejaré que lleves esto a otro acantilado solo para verla caer."

His face paled, and Amy grabbed him some water. This was more than the food making him sick.

A voice boomed from the phone. "Se que mataste al orto."

"I'll be back," he said to Amy. He left her, glass of water in hand, and she felt the need for a glass of wine. She sipped it, listening to music, and worked on deep cleaning the house. Anything to occupy her mind.

Hours and a bottle of wine later, her phone rang. "Hello?" she answered.

"It's your tia."

"What?" She tried to place the voice. *So tia doesn't mean good. What else am I missing?*

"The auntie," the voice explained. "Auntie Rose?"

"Oh, hello! Have you seen Tommy? He left in a rush, and I think he went over to your place?" Amy placed the face, just barely. She was one of the women at the table who'd refused to make conversation.

"Look, I overheard the conversation between his mom and him. You should know that he had a wife once, before you. He took her on a hike, and she fell and died. And well, it was strange. I don't wanna spread rumors but—"

"Say that again?" Amy's mind went fuzzy.

"Something wasn't right. Tommy's mama didn't want you to go with him."

"Go where?" Amy asked, sitting down, hoping the dizziness was the wine.

"On the hike. You know, by the water."

"So she messed with the food? To keep me from going with Tommy?" She let her back rest against the wall and slid to the floor, but not before she locked the door. "Why?"

There was a pause on the line as her mother-in-law yelled something in Spanish. Rose translated in a quiet voice. "She said she knows he killed the other one."

16

GRANDPA'S GUN

He snuck the box into his room. Grandpa knew, of course he knew, but he acted like he didn't. He just told the boy to keep the varmints in the box until they were big enough to release. They were little rabbits this time. The boy found them in the field and waited for days for their mama to come and get them. But she never did, so he put them in that little shoebox and gave them water and milk through a little water dropper. He picked grass and wrapped them in an old blanket to keep them warm. He'd run home from school and pick the best flowers and leaves to drop in their box, a taste of the outside.

Grandpa told him it was time; he grew meaner the older the rabbits got. He'd slapped the boy for wasting milk, and the next day when the boy came home from school, a bushel of weeds in hand, he discovered an empty box.

Grandpa slurred his words, "They were too old, and

you know it. I warned you."

The boy knew he'd waited too long. But he soon found baby birds. He smuggled them in the house and poked holes in the top of the box when they were nearly big enough to jump out. He was going to release them. But he waited too long, and Grandpa got mad at their chirps and stomped the box flat. But Grandpa was nice after that.

So, the boy went in search of something else. He found some mice. Grandpa wouldn't like those, but Grandpa was happy for now. For a time. But when the rage and anger grew and bubbled at the surface, Grandpa took the box the mice were sleeping in and tossed them in the toilet.

The boy couldn't get any more critters after that. He had a kitten for a moment, but he liked her too much, so he hid her away in the neighbor's barn. He saw her, from time to time, out in the field catching butterflies.

But Grandpa got mad again and slapped the boy across the cheek for stealing his boots. Grandpa took his gun, the one that always hung by the front door, and marched outside. A shot reverberated through the wide, open plains.

It was the family dog this time. The outside one, the old mutt Grandpa kept around to warn him of the neighbors and coyotes.

So, the boy went and found some more baby birds, and he hid them under his bed, just where Grandpa would know where to look. That way, next time Grandpa got angry, he wouldn't point the gun at the boy. He'd have baby birds to step on.

INDIE AUTHORS NEED YOU!

Thank you so much for reading this book of strange stories! Reviews help more than you realize, so if you'd be willing, pop on over to wherever you purchased this book, and leave your review there. It would mean the world to me, thank you!

ACKNOWLEDGMENTS

There were so many people (and things) who had a hand in this book. I have been compiling this collection over the last year and not many people were aware of my intentions of creating a strange book of creepy fiction, but now is my chance to thank them.

First, I would like to thank my husband, Malachi. You got to hear me read a few early versions of some stories and were always willing to offer feedback. You are the biggest supporter of what I do, thank you!

To my dad, Chris, for reading some early versions of these stories and your willingness to read more, even after you needed "to take a shower after that one story." Sorry it made you feel gross (not really).

To my mom, Mindy, because you are my mom and I love you. But I KNOW these stories are not your cup of tea... I will not be offended if you just pretend to have read this strange little book.

To my in-laws, I am one of the few who can they not

only love their in-laws, but they actually *like* them! John and Luvonne, your support (even though you really didn't know what I was writing) means a lot more than you know.

To my sisters, Cassidy and Jordan, thank you for inspiring some of these horrific tales. Just kidding! (Or am I...?)

To my brothers, Anthony and Zach, you little men are terrifying in your own special way. Your new (legal) ability to drive has given me a lot to think about when it comes to life and near-death experiences. For that, thank you for the inspiration.

To Kent Shawn, thank you for reading some weird and early versions of stories and giving me pointed and blunt (and painful) feedback. It was more appreciated than you realize!

To my dear friends, Isaiah, Morgan, Ashton, Eli, Jahsh (not a typo), Kendra, Mark, Carley, Anice, Emily, Ashlyn and Suey. Most of you didn't get a chance to read anything I wrote, but your constant support and encouragement really kept me going when, more often than not, it felt like I was shouting into the void. But you heard me and let me know.

To my beta readers, Kent Shawn (again), Hannah R. Palmer, Victoria Wren, Orla Hart, and Richard Holliday, you all are the best writer friends, though we have never actually met face to face, (bless this thing called the internet). You are my writer people. (If you, reader, want some great reads in the future, you should check these people out!)

To my cover designer (Qamber Designs) and editor

(Katie Wismer). You both made my book come alive and I cannot thank you enough.

To the many glasses of coffee, whiskey, and wine. To the long walks in alleyways and the beach, and to the insomnia. You also made this possible, in some way or another, and I don't know if I should thank you or condemn you. Probably both.

To you, my reader, for making it to the end of this strange little book. Thank you.

ABOUT THE AUTHOR

Bethany Votaw started writing in college on little notecards in an effort to stay awake during chemistry. If you can't find her, she is probably taking a nap on the beach or playing in a river.

Her work has been published in *Everyday Fiction*, *The Book Smuggler's Den*, *42 Word Anthology*, and many other fine journals.

Feel free to follow her on Instagram @bethanyjvotaw (where she tries to post regularly) or on Twitter @bethanyvotaw (where she posts nonsense) or sign up for her newsletter at www.bethanyjvotaw.com (where she sends important monthly updates and secret stories).

COPYRIGHT

Paperback ISBN 978-1-7365636-3-2

eBook ISBN 978-1-7365636-2-5

First paperback edition June 2021

Cover art by Qamber Designs

Interior illustrations by Bethany Votaw

Author Photo by Morgan Votaw with Refine Social Studios